Books should be returned or renewed by the
last date stamped above

_____

_____

_____

THE RENEGADE

John Prescott

CHIVERS
THORNDIKE

This Large Print book is published by BBC Audiobooks Ltd, Bath, England and by Thorndike Press®, Waterville, Maine, USA.

Published in 2006 in the U.K. by arrangement with Golden West Literary Agency.

Published in 2006 in the U.S. by arrangement with Golden West Literary Agency.

U.K. Hardcover   ISBN 10: 1–4056–3860–5   (Chivers Large Print)
                 ISBN 13: 978 1 405 63860 9
U.K. Softcover   ISBN 10: 1–4056–3861–3   (Camden Large Print)
                 ISBN 13: 978 1 405 63861 6
U.S. Softcover   ISBN 0–7862–8858–2 (British Favorites)

The text of this Large Print edition is unabridged.
Other aspects of the book may vary from the original edition.

Set in 16 pt. New Times Roman.

Printed in Great Britain on acid-free paper.

British Library Cataloguing in Publication Data available

Library of Congress Cataloging Number: 2006020794

1

Las Vegas of a summer noon possessed the sharp lines of a dry-point landscape when the Santa Fe chuffed in and Clay Forrest stepped down from the coach and saw Ygenio Jaramillo waiting for him with the roan horse strung on a lead behind his own. For a moment he had the notion that nothing had changed at all, and that those three years passed over in time had been products of his imagination. The roan horse looked pretty much as he always had—the clean, red form and radiant coat—and Ygenio had not altered either. Except for his attitude of caution, occasioned by the nature of the day, Ygenio was no different than he had been at any time before.

Ygenio blew his nose violently between his fingers, and shook Clay's hand with heartiness.

'Clay! Clay, how are you? Clay, you look like a million brand-new pesos! On the railroad you come, and we are waiting for you here.'

'It's all right,' Clay said. 'It's all right, Ygenio.'

'*Como no*, it is *bueno* for certain. We are here, yes, and now we are all together and going home. Regard the Morgan—see how he

1

is happy to see you.'

'It's all right,' Clay said again. 'Don't get so damned excited. Everything's all right, Ygenio.'

Clay let Ygenio's hand slip from his own, and moved closer to the roan horse. For a number of seconds, the Morgan looked at him, then it dipped its head and blew softly on his hands. The warm velvet nuzzled his palms in tentative inhalations and Clay's mind turned back to the memory of other days. He tried to think how long ago Pa had given him this animal. Four years? No, three and a half was closer to it, but it seemed nearer a lifetime now; yet his recollection of the occasion was as clear and fresh, and unclouded by intervening incidents, as though it had happened but an hour ago. Never had there been a fine red horse like this one; unless it was the one that Pa himself had ridden at his death.

Clay rubbed the long bones of the arched nose, slapped the solid neck, and went around the side and tugged at the latigo. He turned the tap, put his foot into the stirrup and swung on up; and grinned as he felt the solid leather smack his backsides.

'I reckon that's pretty damned good, now, ain't it?' he said to Ygenio. 'I been needin' somethin' like this.'

Ygenio was laughing loudly as he threw his leg across the cantle. '*Si*, you look fine, Clay.

2

You look like a great *rico* upon that horse. Only before I come up here from the ranch I say to Apolinaria, I say, "That Clay, that young *señor*, he will be the greatest *caballero* in the whole of New Mexico upon that horse. Ho! How he will look!"'

Clay rode a few yards down the white street before he said anything. He'd been working this thing out ever since he'd got on the train to come back home; he had it pretty straight in his own mind, and he might just as well get it that way in Ygenio's now, before they went any further. There was no sense in dilly-dallying around with it. He couldn't have Ygenio carrying on like a kid, behaving like he never had before. It was a strain on both of them.

'You can take it easy now, Ygenio,' he said. 'It's all right, you can quiet down. You don't have to tear your head off like that. I'm a jailbird; you know it, and I know it, so let's get used to it and be natural. It's three years out of my life and I'm willing to forget it and take up where I left off. Savvy?'

Ygenio relieved himself of a large breath of air.

'I savvy, Clay. *Si*, I understand how it is. I simply want you to feel good inside. I want you to know I am glad to see you again.'

Clay slowed down to let Ygenio come abreast of him.

'I know you're glad to see me, and I

appreciate it. I guess there's nothin' in the world like friends, and there wouldn't be much point in coming back if you and Apolinaria weren't around. But don't go worrying about it; I feel good, all right.'

Clay felt clumsy explaining this, and he experienced a sense of relief when Ygenio appeared to recognize it and accept what he said. Ygenio smiled again, and Clay knew that he had put it right.

'Now, then,' he said, on a new slant of thought. 'How's it back home? Apolinaria ain't losin' any weight, is she?'

Ygenio laughed with no sound, gently. 'No, she will never lose weight. She is very well. And busy. She is always busy.'

'I guess you get enough to eat, then. You look healthy.'

'Oh, yes, I am very healthy. There is plenty.'

There was a silence while Ygenio arranged his thoughts. 'Clay, one of Apolinaria's relatives from White Oaks has come to stay. She has trouble in her family, but she will return again, soon.' It was spoken as a statement, but there was a question in it.

'That's all right,' Clay said. 'It makes no difference.' He didn't think about it; his mind was already beyond it. 'What about the rest of it?'

Ygenio adjusted his soiled sombrero carefully. 'Well, you know what Apolinaria writes to you before. It is the same again this

4

year. I have trouble because I cannot get the men to help. There are some cattle missing, and there are not as many calves as we should have.'

'Rustling?' Clay said.

'I do not think so,' Ygenio said. 'It is mostly because there is no one to help. I have one or two, maybe three sometimes, but they do not stay long; and anyway, they are not the ones to have for long. I do my best, Clay, but you know how it can be.'

Clay spoke without looking at Ygenio. His eyes were rambling from side to side along the street, passing from this weathered building front to that. He'd been in this town before, but now everything looked drowsy and without energy in the sun and stillness of the day; not like he'd remembered it. Down the street, a young boy, maybe twelve or fourteen, was puddling in the dust with his bare feet, and watching them as they came along; a solitary sign of life in the heat and quiet.

'I thought we was agreed we was goin' to speak right out, with none of this fancy footwork,' Clay said. 'What you mean is, you can't get nobody to work on the place 'cause everyone knows it's Forrest property and their minds is set against us.'

'Well, I do not like to say that right out, Clay, but that may have something to do with it, I think.' Ygenio looked quickly into Clay's face, as though to soften the reality of what he

5

said.

'Well, you got to be direct about it,' Clay said. 'We ain't goin' to get anywhere 'less you recognize what's what. In the eyes of them on the Pecos I'm a criminal and there ain't no good comin' in failin' to meet it that way.'

'I do not think you are bad.' Ygenio spoke in a subdued tone, quietly. 'The trial, it was wrong, and you are not bad.'

'Well, I know I ain't neither,' Clay said. 'But I thought a lot on it, and I figure the best thing is to let things be and to hell with what people think. No amount of talk or denial is goin' to change anything. There's that other business, anyway; that Moore business. They ain't goin' to forget I rode with him, not with him still rippin' up the Territory.'

Clay turned slightly in his saddle when he said this, and he was startled by the cast of Ygenio's face. It made him feel a slow wonder at the great capacity for loyalty in the Spaniard; it made him think there weren't many who'd put up with what Ygenio had in the years since Hardin Forrest's death. The Pecos people didn't take kindly to a man who handled the affairs of a convicted criminal.

Clay worked a note of kindness into his tone to cover up the brittle feeling in him. 'I expect Moore and some of his has been around. They been causing trouble in the valley?'

'No, there is no trouble,' Ygenio said. 'But

6

they come and ask for you. They come and ask, and they go away again.'

'They ain't been foolin' with the stock, have they?'

'No, I do not think they do that,' Ygenio said. 'But the people in the valley, the people, when they learn that Moore and his *compadres* come to the ranch, are angry; and they say bad things of you again.'

Clay glared at the white dust boiling around the red roan's hooves. 'Let 'em,' he said. 'Let 'em say what they damned well please; yeah, and let 'em think it, too.'

That time there was a dense quiet between them, and they were nearly to the place where the young boy was lounging against the gallery post of one of the gray, tired buildings, when Ygenio regarded Clay apologetically.

'Clay,' he began, 'Clay, maybe it is best to sell your place. Apolinaria and I will stay with you and work for you as we did for your father, and you know that, but it will not be a happy place for you with the feeling like it is. There are those, I think, who would like your land, and would pay for it if you would sell it. The Señor Liston one time declares he would give a good price.'

Clay laughed without humor. 'Dodge Liston, huh? Good old self-righteous Dodge. Pious-speakin' goat.'

Ygenio massaged his saddle horn with his hand. '*Si*, yes, he is a great one with words and

7

large thoughts, but he would pay for the land, and that is something.'

'With all the money and land he's already got, he still wants more,' Clay said. 'Some ain't never satisfied, I guess.'

Clay was looking ahead again. He was watching the boy against the gallery post, and he saw that the youngster's attitude of indolence was gone, and that he was regarding them in an attentive and wary way. He was nothing more than a sandy-haired sprout, gangling and kind of gawky, the way that kids get at that age, but there was a special kind of caution in his manner that Clay remembered people having when they knew they were watching him. Clay's horse was nearly broadside on to the boy when he suddenly turned and shouted into the doorway in back of him.

'Hey! It's Clay Forrest! The Moore gang's here! Clay Forrest's ridin' in and the Moore gang's here! Gawd-almighty, he's comin' down the street!'

Clay felt his insides jerk. The shock of it went through him to his boots, and jelled in quick, cold panic. He wanted to run, to fly, to cut loose and ride like crazy beyond the sound of that piping voice. Out of that town and away and on and on until the roan horse fell exhausted. Beside him, Ygenio swore, ranged up close and brought his gun out, then let it drop again as Clay brought his hand across his wrist. The panic had gone as quickly as it had come, and Clay sat poker-straight as the Vegas people bobbed their heads through doors and windows.

'Look at him!' A voice called from an upstairs window. 'Forrest! By God, it is Forrest!'

'See him, honey? Right there! On that red horse!'

A buxom woman scuttled across the road, her feet impelled by terror. A saloon swamper came through his batwings to slop the boardwalk, caught the warning cry, and disappeared again. And down a side street the voice of the boy was chanting in a high, shrill wail. 'The Moore gang is here! The killers have come!'

On a gallery roof, the querulous voice of an old man, brash in his senility, picked it up. 'Clay Forrest is ridin' in! The murderin' scum is here for sure!'

'*Sapristi!*' Ygenio said. 'These goats! I tell them! I will teach them manners!'

'No, you won't,' Clay said. 'You keep out of this. It's me they're talkin' about.'

He jerked around again. He saw the bobbing heads and vacant, moving faces—the expressions of apprehension and secret enjoyment and morbid curiosity and anticipation, hoping, fearing, waiting. He saw them all at once and they were all the same, primitive and animal. It made him take a kind

9

of fierce twisted pleasure in the sensation he was creating. It made him almost wish that everything they said was true. It made him laugh and shout and yell abuse at them.

'You're damned right, it's Clay Forrest! I'm ridin' through your stinkin' rat hole and there ain't a man among you that can stop me! I'll take you yellow-bellies ten at a time, and the rest of you can have the carrion!'

Clay swung around, ripped his jacket off and waved it overhead. The hot, crazy madness was slamming in his head and he couldn't stop it now. Everything was there in an eruption of long-gone bitter things restored to life with hate and passion—the black days of the Lincoln fight, the tragic death of Hardin, the rapacity of Robey Moore, and the endless months in prison for a crime he hadn't done. It was all together, one with the other, inseparable.

'Look here!' he yelled. 'See? I ain't even got a gun! You know why? I don't need one, that's why! I don't need one 'cause I can kill with my eyes!'

They were crazy and insane, the things he said, but so was everything.

2

They took their time going from Las Vegas to the plainslands on the lower Pecos. They took their time and Clay was in no particular hurry because he had long since rejected hurry as a way to anything. It never seemed to pay to do more than take things as they came.

They rode through fine country in those days. They rode through high grasslands and deep *vegas*, across the generous flanks of hills, and irrigated valleys green with water and lush with promise. They rode through towns and villages—Les Montoyas, Anton Chico—and others, nameless, sleeping in the sun, where antique 'dobes gave a look of age at one with the land itself. They followed the river into the southern plains through spreading flats of memory and old associations.

They passed beneath the barracks of old Fort Sumner, and beyond the town where Billy Bonney, alias Antrim, alias the Kid, lay sleeping in the dust. Bonney, yes, and Charlie Bowdre, too. And Tom O'Folliard; Pat Garret's craftsmanship. Times had changed in the years that Clay had been away, and law and order reigned. It gave him a queer feeling to remember he'd sometimes ridden in the Lincoln County war beside those men; like other hired gunmen, they'd turned desperado when the fight had ended.

Below Fort Sumner they bent due south and left the river for a while. They'd been on the move for most of four days and they were getting into country which had the smell of home about it. Far to the west and southwest, the Capitans and Sacramentos crashed their peaks against the sky and filled Clay with the renewed wonder of their creation; and with the old unhappy contemplation of the events which had taken place within their lifting shadows. Most of all the grief and trouble in his life had developed in those mountains.

Within a country courthouse shielded by their slopes a circuit-riding judge had sent him off to prison. And within their pine-shot bellies his pa had gone down and died.

As the *antiguos* told it, those whose age allowed them a memory of distant times, there was the Pecos war, the Harrold war, and finally the most far-reaching and violent of all, the Lincoln war. The first had developed in the early Seventies after John Chisum had brought his Long Rail and Jingle Bob brands up the lower Pecos cattle trails from the heart of Texas and turned his animals loose upon the open plains for any enterprising long rope to gather in. The second assumed the aspect of a personal vendetta wherein the vicious, ranging Harrold brothers from the southern Pecos had engaged in sporadic but vindictive warfare with the Lincoln townsmen. Because

12

the first two ran nearly together in time and place the line of separation blurred and obscured itself in men's minds, and at the end of nearly a decade of upheaval they were consumed in the greater and final convulsion which men had come to call the Lincoln County war.

That one Clay remembered well. If the other two were softened by his childhood memories, the big one retained the sharp and definite lines of a steel engraving.

In the beginning there was the town of Lincoln, deep in the bosom of the Capitans. There was Lincoln, and beyond it, in a folding of the blue and wooded hills there was Fort Stanton, where a portion of the California Column had been posted and had mustered out. New Mexico was an old land turned new again, with the Civil War behind, with the Anglo coming in to settle and the Indians mostly quited; and a smart man could see the possibilities. Some of those California volunteers had not gone home again.

So, then, as Clay had heard it told, there eventually came to Lincoln the trio Murphy, Dolan and Riley, and there arose the Big Store among the Spanish *casas*, so-called not only for its grandiose magnificence, but also for the fact that nothing could compare with its variety of provender for more than a hundred miles around. One could go to Santa Fe, and away beyond, men said, before one found an establishment stocked so well as Murphy's place. In fact, a good many folks who made their regular or irregular journeys to Santa Fe and other centers abandoned these more distant points and changed their trading habits.

Lincoln in the Capitans became an island of material plenty in a sea of grass that stretched from Raton Pass to the Big Bend of the Rio Grande.

L. G. Murphy, former major with the California Column, became a power in the country. His name achieved the familiarity of a household word throughout the thirty thousand square miles that lay in Lincoln County. More so than his associates, he attained a celebrated prominence; under his direction the Big Store flourished.

With a nose for money, he caused the enterprise to enter other fields. A feed mill was established, and a brewery. He secured the beef contracts at Fort Stanton and the Mescalero Agency where the Apaches had been rounded up. He organized a loan and banking service. The prices on the Big Store items were enormous, but a man could get the money through a stock loan, simply for the asking. Whisky was supplied in generous quantity to make decision easy.

He entered politics and made himself a probate judge. He arranged for law enforcement. The shadow of the House, as

14

the name evolved to be, fell long upon the Territory. If a man got squeezed on a House loan, or became outspoken concerning treatment he'd received, certain young men with old faces might pay a call on him one day. Here and there, ranchers left the country, ruined; others simply disappeared. The holdings of the House expanded, and the young-old men rode far and wide. Strange, out-country brands showed up on the contract beef. Folks began to wonder where some of that beef was coming from.

Clay's pa one time said, 'This can't go on forever. Murphy's runnin' this county like it was a European duchy. He thinks he's a goddammed king or something.'

A good many people thereabouts considered Hardin Forrest a fool for speaking out thuswise, and pretty near an idiot later on when he got entangled in it. Clay sometimes wondered if there might not have been an element of truth in these surface estimations, but then he would feel ashamed at having such a thought because his pa was a strong man, a free man, who had definite ideas as to what was right and what was wrong; he was never a fool when it came to righteousness or morals. It was black or white with him, and never gray.

He was a good man, Hardin Forrest, stern when the need arose, uncompromising on points of principle, but kindly, too, by nature.

He kept good cattle and horses, and treated them with consideration. He would spend a winter's night, if need be, raking the chaparral for a strayed-off calf, or hand-feed a sick colt back to health. He was a pious man in his fashion, and Clay remembered his reading to them from the family Bible by the light of an oil lamp in the home ranch near Roswell. But his religion was a strong one, self-respecting, a both-feet-on-the-ground business with him, and was not composed of fawning supplications. He was Missouri-bred and he had powerful convictions in his heart.

In those days they lived beneath the reaching shadow of the House in the mountains to the west. One time Hardin sold a steer lot to the Murphy men, but he was never paid. Other men had taken that treatment lying down, but Hardin had a spine as rigid as a bayonet. He bided his time, and when the trouble broke, he threw in with the opposition.

*   *   *

'Now, we're goin' to see something, all right.'

Funny how words stuck in a man's mind sometimes. Clay remembered Hardin speaking out that way, and the way he stood, even, rocking on his heels a little on the gallery of the ranch house when they'd learned how Murphy's style was being

16

trimmed at long last.

Hardin had now been dead beyond three years, but he always came alive again for Clay whenever those words would cross his mind. They somehow stayed on the edge of it now as he and Ygenio rode the warm days through, coming down from Vegas. It seemed as if his being nearer to the home range, nearer to the source of all those old events and tragedies, had endowed them with a new existence, resurrected-like.

John Tunstall and McSween—Alexander, his first name was—were a strange pair to come upon the country. The first was an Englishman who settled in the hills upon a ranch near Lincoln, and Clay remembered seeing him a time or two, his pleasant beefy face, and the simple way of him. The other was a lawyer from the East, a sober, learned man, of a religious turn of mind. Folks said he'd one time studied for the clergy.

Tongues wagged and heads nodded at the style of living the McSweens seemed to be accustomed to. It was a strange sight to see the outland woman traipsing in her brocades past the dusky, sandaled *mujers* up in Lincoln. When her piano came by horse and wagon all the way from Trinidad the event became a matter of historical importance.

As Hardin said, 'They were going to see something, all right.'

It wasn't long before Tunstall and the

lawyer took a shine to one another and entered business for themselves. The way Clay had it, McSween first spent some time working for the House, but he had a falling out with Murphy, and he and Tunstall went into competition with it. Murphy wasn't the only one who'd seen the possibilities in the country.

To hear it told, the business prospered from the start. If folks didn't comprehend McSween, they found the affable Tunstall to their liking. They didn't find themeslves hard pressed for any loan he might have made them. A man could buy the things he needed without puttin' his soul upon the line to bind the deal. No one braced him up with whisky and tried to skin him. The word went out that life at the House had ceased to be the free and easy thing it used to be. Tunstall and McSween were making inroads on the long prosperity Murphy's company had enjoyed. There was even talk of a beef contract at the Fort and Indian Agency for the *nueves*.

There was talk of strain and trouble, too.

There was a lot of it that Clay and a good many others never got the straight of. There seemed to be some legal aspects to the picture. Gossips pondered a rumor concerning the juggling of the House books to show McSween as owing a large sum from the time of his previous employ. Wise men, safely distant from the rumblings, opined that

Murphy's whisky-hospitality had got the better of his own self. He was a sick man, that was known, beset by more harassments than met the eye. It was understood his bankers up in Santa Fe had become alarmed at the failing state of business, at the number of blotted brands that filled the beef contracts. John Chisum was said to be whetting a knife at his Bosque Grande ranch.

McSween and Tunstall might well have been the source of a number of Murphy's ills, but they served him handily as scapegoats, too. Murphy was a plotter and a diplomat, but he could be a man of action just as well. In this extremity he worked his wrath upon his competition. One day he sent Billy Morton and a bunch to Tunstall's Feliz ranch, south of Lincoln. The purpose of these men was not made clear when they set out, but later on Dick Brewer, Tunstall's foreman, and a child-faced puncher known around as Billy Bonney found their employer lying in the road. His brains were splattered in the dust; his hat was neatly folded underneath his head.

From then on it was a matter of choosing sides. The County was split wide open and any man could understand it. Involvement became a matter of course for many of those that Murphy had wronged and another surge of young-old men came loping through the country, seeking gunman's pay. They came from far and wide, and this time they weren't all riding for the House.

Hardin was no gun hand, no professional, as so many of the new ones were, but he vowed to side against the Murphy crowd, with those avenging Tunstall's wanton slaughter. For a time he rode with Brewer's posse, leg and leg with some of the hardest men in that or any other country. He shared his jerky with the likes of Tom Hill, John Middleton, Dave Rudabaugh, Doc Skurlock, Bowdre, O'Folliard, Ike Stockton and the blue-eyed Billy Bonney. The issues were being submerged in the drench of blood, the pall of burning powder, but Hardin rode for right and justice. He always kept his Bible with him; he never got confused.

A while later, Clay remembered, Robey Moore came on the dodge from the south of Texas and hired himself to the highest bidder. He was as handy with a gun as a man can be and Hardin Forrest was shrewd enough to recognize it. Without changing loyalties in the cause, he switched to Robey's newly organized contingent. He knew Robey was a money fighter, with not a care for the principles involved, but he knew he was good life insurance, too.

And about that time he bought the Morgans and gave Clay to understand that he could ride with them if he so chose. Clay'd reached eighteen years upon that day, and he was still too young to understand the tangled web he wove. Even could he see ahead to what the future held, to the dark camps and the long night trails, to senseless slaughter that continued between those purely outlaw after Tunstall, Murphy and the other principals were dead, to his own self being framed for murder, he would have done it anyway.

As long as he was riding, he rode like Hardin, in the right. But a week from the day he joined, Hardin dragged his last breath from the pine-braced air of the Ruidoso country, and Clay was all alone. But he had signed with Robey Moore for better or for worse.

*   *   *

Clay always remembered the day that Hardin died. For beauty, the untempered air of the Ruidoso timber had no peer in his mind or memory, and its splendor was at its most compelling on that fatal day. They had kept a cold camp on property owned jointly by Charlie Bowdre and Doc Skurlock, and they were awake and on the lookout as dawn washed red and gold among the trees about them. They were anticipating trouble.

Hardin had put the Morgans into hobbles for the night and Clay went out to bring them in. There had been none awake but himself and Diamond-Back, the night guard, when he went out, but coming back he saw them all stretching out of sleep and getting ready for

21

what they knew was coming.

'I figure these two will prove their worth this day,' Hardin said as Clay brought the horses in and got ready to saddle up. Hardin stood there in his long underwear and trousers and boots and his face had a clean-cut, steady look about it, even through the growth of whiskers. 'You scared, son?'

Clay was deliberate with putting the bit into the roan's mouth. 'I guess I'm scared, all right, but I ain't scared in a way that'd make me run off.'

'That's all right, then,' Hardin said. 'If you'd told me you wasn't I'd of known you was lyin'. Every man's scared the first time.'

'You think there's goin' to be something big, Pa?' Clay asked. Clay kept busy with the saddle and harness and tried to be casual.

'Can't say for sure just yet, but Robey's got the feel for it. Stands to reason, though, that Murphy's bunch ain't goin' to let us sashay out of here without something. Not after what was done to Billy Morton for killin' Tunstall.'

Clay turned around and looked at Hardin. Hardin's whiskers had a high shine in the sun coming through the trees. 'We didn't have nothin' to do with Morton,' Clay said. 'That was Skurlock and Bowdre and that Bonney feller they call the Kid.'

'It don't make any difference, Clay,' Hardin said. 'It's all the same. We're all in it together.'

Pretty soon they had the horses and gear

ready and Robey came back from scouting around and they all talked it over. He'd had Ed Picket out there with him and they'd spotted the Murphy bunch working up the creek from over east. They'd likely come out in a wide arc from Lincoln, Robey said, and was figuring to come upon them in surprise.

The thing about Robey Moore was in his face. He wasn't much to look at otherwise. He was kind of sloppy in his dress and manner, never cleaned up very much, or shaved or anything like that, and didn't look so very different from anybody else. But when you looked him in the face you got a kind of chill inside. Some folks said a man's eyes was the windows to his soul, but if that was true, then Robey didn't have no soul. His eyes was as empty and vacant as a dried-out well.

After Robey told them what was up, and said they'd split and take the Murphy bunch from either side they broke it up and climbed aboard. Bob Fergus and Ed Picket and Diamond-Back and Steve Howard were going to go around and stir things up when the Murphy men came up.

'I figure you Forrests better stay with me,' Robey said when they were ready. Robey swung his eyes around the small clearing they had camped in, then took a long look at Clay. Clay hitched at his belt.

'How you feel, kid?' Robey said.

Clay sat straight in the saddle and ran his

23

hand along the roan's neck. 'Why, I guess I feel pretty good. How do you feel?'

Robey allowed himself a dry laugh, and looked around some more. Robey was always looking around, like he suspected every sound and motion in the brush.

'You sound spunky, all right,' he said then. 'Hope you show like you talk.'

'I won't turn tail, if that's what you mean.'

'You just do what you're told and everything'll be all right.'

'I figure I can do that,' Clay said. He wished to hell they'd get through gabbing and get on with it. It made him feel peculiar that Robey should put this talk at him and examine him this way at such a time.

'All right, then,' Robey said, 'we better git.'

They rode on out. At the edge of the clearing the waiting party crossed the Ruidoso and went into the trees on the other side. Clay followed his pa and Robey up the bank and then they made a big turn and doubled back down below the place where they had camped. They were going directly into the big, gold sun and Clay had never seen a thing like that before. The whole forest was filled with color and the carpet was soft and spongy underfoot. In the high trees the birds were calling and scampering here and there, and not far off the creek was splashing and spilling over the rocks in drops and streaks of copper. It made him want to go right over there and get the feel of it around his feet and ankles.

In a little bit Robey went ahead to look around and Clay picked up his gait so he could ride beside his pa. They went in quiet for a spell and then Hardin commenced to talk.

'You stick with Robey and you'll be all right,' he said. 'Should anything happen, you stick with him 'til this is done. Then there'll be the ranch for you.'

Clay felt something get under his back and make him sit straighter. It wasn't the kind of tone Hardin normally used, except when he might be reading from the Bible, and it made him take a slow, sidewise look at him.

'Why, I reckon I am stickin' with him, ain't I?' he said. 'We both are.'

'Sure, I know we are, but just the same, you do like I say. You stick with him. He'll get you through this if anybody can. He may be just another hired gun-slinger to a lot of folks, and maybe his end'll be like all the others, but I figure he'll last through this business.'

Clay turned it over in his head and tried to work it out. It seemed almost like Hardin was slipping away from him, going off to a place that he couldn't trail him to, but there was no time to explore all the implications because Robey came busting back to them through the trees and reined up in a flurry in front of them.

'Dammit,' Robey said, 'they're on to it. We

25

got to work this different. They split up just like we did. We got to get back to the others. Come on, let's go!' Robey's gelding danced and shied and Robey called across his shoulder as he sank the spurs in deep. 'Come on, dammit, let's go! Let's go!'

The shooting broke out before they'd gone a hundred yards and Clay could hear it booming and echoing among the trees ahead of them. He was pressed warm against the soft coat of the roan's neck and the muscles underneath him spread and expanded against his chest, and against his face when he would put it there. In between the shooting bursts he could hear the soft pounding of the roan's hooves on the ground beneath, and sometimes those of Robey's horse beyond him, and those of Hardin to the rear.

When the split part of the Murphy crowd stumbled onto them Clay was not aware of it until he heard the sudden sound of the close-in gunfire and the blending scream of the Morgan that his pa rode. Then it hit him all at once and he was conscious of the shadows racing through the trees to the side and rear, of the ragged streaks of flame bursting bright and vivid against the green and brown, and of Hardin spilling to the ground beneath his horse.

Clay swung his own around without knowing he had done it and sent it crashing back toward Hardin. Vaguely above the sound of gunfire he heard Robey yelling profanely at him, but he kept on going back. He was close to Hardin now. He could see how he was pinned and how he was wrenching at his gun. The Morgan heaved and jerked in agony and each movement of the heavy animal brought a lighter shade of gray to Hardin's features.

The other rider exploded through the brush as Clay was swinging down. Clay saw the double-barreled shotgun spring from the saddle scabbard and he felt the sickest, coldest fear he ever knew engulf him as the yawning muzzles smashed their lead and fire into Hardin's tossing body. He saw the brown, young face and eyes as thin as leaves of grass behind the polished stock, and then he saw those same eyes splash red and messy as the slugs from his revolver tore the rider from his saddle and hammered him into the ground and its soft pine-needle covering. Clay thumbed the hammer of the fat Colt in a roar and sheet of flame and when it was empty and clicking dry he raised the gun and pistol-whipped the body at his feet. He was still standing there, numb and half-senseless, when Robey swung up and threw himself upon him.

'I thought I told you to come with me!' Robey Moore was shouting at him, halfway screaming. 'I thought you was goin' to do like I say! What you doin' here?'

The things that Robey said did not register with Clay and he could only gape at him like someone who was listening to a foreign tongue. He felt like he was made of wood or stone and when his arm moved in an indefinite arc toward Hardin's body it did not seem to belong to him at all. Even when Robey hit him he didn't feel it; or when he glanced against the giant pine, and rolled on the ground and pushed drunkenly to his hands and knees.

And over and over, the fine, clean air of the Ruidoso timber carried the insensate rage of Robey's voice.

'I'll learn yuh, Forrest! I'll learn yuh to do what I say! I'll learn yuh who gives orders in this bunch! God damn, you ain't never goin' to let it slip your mind again!'

3

On the seventh day from Vegas, Ygenio and Clay pulled over the slow rise above the Forrest land and buildings and eased their horses toward the spreading cottonwoods, strong and fertile in a long lane extending from the dooryard. A slow catch came into Clay's throat when they turned into it and he saw the shapeless and attentive Apolinaria shading her eyes toward them from the gallery at the far end. She gave a low cry as the two animals came out of the lane and walked through the sun of the court, and half-dragged Clay from the saddle when they stopped at last.

'*Caramba*, Señor Clay! Clay, you are skin and bones! They have starved you near to death in that place!'

'No, they ain't, Apolinaria. No, they ain't,' Clay said. 'It wasn't that bad.' He laughed self-consciously into Apolinaria's round face and felt the clean warmth of home coming into him again.

'It is so,' Apolinaria said with insistence. Her strong, splayed fingers explored his ribs, picked at his arms and thighs. 'Look! Observe! Your shanks are bare! Bare as a picked shoat. You are naked!'

Clay evaded Apolinaria's prowling hands and commenced to remove the saddle and blanket from the horse. 'I ain't neither naked,' he said. 'I even growed some in that place. I stretched out. I just ain't so fat and kidlike any more.'

'No, it is food you need; I can tell. Ygenio, you fool of all the fools; why did you not feed him? You bring him home like a shadow!'

Ygenio slung his saddle on the tie-rail. 'What should I do, push the food into his throat with my fist? He eats what he pleases. Who will do more? I think it is as he declares; he is simply more large in some places than before, and not so large in the others.'

'*Madre Dios*, you men, you will be the death

29

of yourselves; the certain death. A blind man could see he is shrinking into the ground.' Apolinaria fixed Clay with a final, compassionate look before returning to the house. 'Food is what he needs. Food! Enchiladas and tortillas and good, hot chili! *Si*, yes, food!'

When Apolinaria had gone Clay set the saddle and other gear on the rail and sent the roan off with a slap on the flank. He took an easy turn around the dooryard, digging his boots into the earth and getting the feel of the place into his body once again. From the rail, Ygenio regarded him with an air of quiet apprehension, as though wondering in his mind what sort of verdict Clay might render on the care the place had had during the years he was away.

Well, Ygenio had done what he could, all right, and Clay could see that no one could have done much better with the kind of transient help he'd had. A man in Ygenio's place couldn't very well look after the herd and buildings, too, and of the whole lot the cattle held the most importance. The buildings could be gotten after now that he was back. They didn't look too bad on casual examination; anyway, not so bad they couldn't be fixed up proper with time and effort.

'You done all right, Ygenio,' Clay said after a time, and Ygenio appeared relieved. 'I guess maybe we can get back on our feet after a bit;

providin' we can get some help out here.'

Ygenio removed his sombrero and slapped the dust out of it against his knee. 'Well, you know what I tell you coming down from Vegas; but we can try.'

'I guess we can do that, all right,' Clay said. 'We'll find someone. I'll get after it right away.' Clay took another slow and easy turn around the court, coming up before Ygenio and twisting his heel into the yielding ground. 'We'll do that pronto. *Muy* pronto.'

They turned the horses into the corral and went inside to eat. If Clay'd doubted the sincerity of Apolinaria's allusions to his health they would have been dispelled, for she piled food upon the table to a point of making it hard for him to find a place to put his elbows. There was everything that he could think of, and prepared in a manner that he hadn't been treated to in a longer stretch of time than he now cared to recall.

Apolinaria had always been relentless in the cooking alcove, and the spread she forced upon them now put Clay in mind of the things which Hardin used to say so long ago.

'You got to watch that Apolinaria, Clay,' he used to say. 'Clay, you got to watch that *mujer* 'less she fill you so you lose the motion of your legs; you're liable to topple right on off your horse some time. She's got a fixation in her head about a man bein' comfortable in his britches. A body just don't look right to that

31

woman 'less he's waddlin' along half-drugged from all that food.'

And Clay knew Hardin had been right. There looked to be no end to all the food Apolinaria had fixed. Every time he dipped his fork into his plate, or scooped a load of chili from the bowl, Apolinaria was right beside him, filling up the dent he'd made; and all the while crowing at him in a tone of impatience and annoyance.

'Eat, skeleton! How can you live if you do not eat? How can you have the strength to lift your hands? Bones! Nothing but bones!'

At last it was done and Clay sank into the hide-backed chair and looked around. He was filled to a point of pain and acute discomfort, but perhaps it served a purpose, for he realized this to be the first time he was wholly relaxed since Ygenio had met him.

As he let his eyes ramble undirected about the large main room the nostalgia of his young life's early memories weighed down upon him. The furnishings of that room had not been altered since the death of his mother in his childhood, and were thus related to his most distant recollections of living in that vast and open country. After she had gone, Hardin had not allowed a single change to be made in their arrangement.

Clay had always understood the reason for this to be based in Hardin's great devotion to her memory, and his desire to be surrounded by those things which had meant life and beauty to her. But he had also come to know in time that Hardin had experienced a sense of guilt at those early hardships and uncertainties which had contributed greatly to her early end, and perhaps that had something to do with it as well.

Except for the wall prints and the tinted china and the needlepoint sofa, and certain now threadbare rugs, which his mother had treasured above all earthly things—and had refused to leave Missouri until they were in the wagon with her—everything else had been made of such native materials as fell to hand.

In that early time, dim and disconnected in Clay's mind, they had whip-sawed pine and cottonwood puncheons for the floors—although Hardin had generally scorned cottonwood as a wood to work with—planks and other pieces for the tables, the chairs, the bedsteads and the doors. Hardin had one time come upon some wormed cedar in the foothills and he had made fine panels for the inner bedroom walls. He had been as proud of those as he had been of the hand-split shingles for the roof, and the fireplace he'd mixed up out of adobe mud and straw.

And everything remained as it had been at the time of its beginning. Even with Hardin gone. Apolinaria saw to that. She had a mystic's respect for the wishes of the dead.

When he thought he could manage it Clay

pulled himself out of the chair and headed toward the dooryard. There was a perilous moment when it appeared that Apolinaria might seize him and force another quart of pinto beans into him, but when her critical scrutiny observed the tight ridges which his Levis made across his belly she smiled with benevolence and let him pass.

Everything was slow and easy in the noontime warmth. The sun was almost directly overhead and the shadows fell in flat pools with no elongation. There was little wind; there was just enough motion to the air to stir the heat and to eliminate discomfort. It was fine and lazy walking through the dooryard.

Before he'd gorged himself on all that food he'd had in mind to take his horse on a slow swing around the place, but that idea did not have much appeal for him just now. So he compromised on a walk around the buildings.

When he heard the short squeal of the pump beyond the gallery of the kitchen door he walked in that direction. It occurred to him he hadn't suitably thanked Apolinaria for her feast and he knew she'd appreciate the gesture. It was his remembrance that she considered simple demolition of her dishes ample expression of enjoyment, but he wanted her to know it had given him special pleasure.

He didn't remember the relative Ygenio had mentioned to him on the way from Vegas until he realized it was not Apolinaria at the pump. By that time he had approached very near to her, and she turned and smiled at him with shyness.

Clay tugged at the sleeve of his shirt. 'Hello,' he said. 'You must be Apolinaria's relative. I'm Clay Forrest.'

'Yes, I know.' The girl's voice was low and warm. 'Apolinaria is my aunt; my father was her brother. I am called Abrana Martinez.'

'That's a nice name,' Clay heard himself saying. 'It's got music to it. Ygenio said you came from White Oaks.'

'Yes, I lived in White Oaks until my father died in the mines up there. When Apolinaria wrote to me I came down here to stay.'

Clay felt compelled to comment on the misfortune, but because she had referred to it simply he decided against it. 'It's nice in White Oaks,' he said instead. 'I've been through there a few times. It's sort of cupped in the mountains, ain't it?' Even though he knew he was being self-conscious talking to this girl it was pleasant and it made him feel good.

'Yes, it is very beautiful in White Oaks,' Abrana Martinez said quietly. 'I am going back there soon, now that you are here again.'

Clay picked up the two wooden buckets, which the girl had filled, and carried them the few feet to the gallery outside the kitchen door.

'Why do you want to go to White Oaks

35

again? Don't you like it here? Is there something for you to do up there?'

Abrana Martinez was watching him. She was standing just beyond the perimeter of shade enveloping the well pump and Clay could see that her hair, which was long with small waves at her shoulders, was not black or blue-black, in the manner of Apolinaria's, but had a rich copper cast, deep in. It did not show in the shade, but was apparent in direct light, and it made him think that her Spanish blood was predominant over any Indian blending.

Her face was like that, too. The coloring was not deep, and the bone structure did not tend toward roundness. Rather, it was oval, and her features were clear and finely proportioned. Her eyes were very black and were accentuated by the light shading of her skin, as were her lips, which were full but not voluptuous. Clay thought she might be seventeen or eighteen, but no more than that.

'I will find something to do,' she said presently. 'There is always something if one looks for it.'

This sounded formal to Clay, and he felt awkward because of it. It made him wonder if she had a personal reason for returning to that place, and it occurred to him that he might have been too forward with his interest. But he didn't want her to leave yet, so he said, 'I want to have a look at my horse; would you come to the corral with me?'

Abrana Martinez smiled carefully, and nodded. 'All right. I do not mind. I can go for only a short time, though, for I must help Apolinaria.'

'That's all right,' Clay said. 'It won't take long. Anyway, you don't want to let her work you to death.'

'She does not do that,' Abrana said. 'She is very kind.'

They were walking toward the pole corral and Clay felt less constrained. Whether this was because they were being impersonal now, or because in going to the horse he was dealing with a familiar thing, he couldn't tell, but he didn't bother to analyze it. It was simply nice being the way they were, and that's all there was about it.

When they came to the corral Abrana placed her arms on one of the rails and rested her chin upon them as she watched the animals inside. Clay stood to one side, and slightly behind her, in such a way that he could see the lines of her neck forming into her shoulders, and the deep cedar glints in her hair, which seemed more striking now that she stood clearly in the boldness of the sun.

'He is very pretty,' Abrana said of the roan horse. 'And noble.'

'Yes,' Clay said. 'He's a Vermont strain. Pa gave him to me for my birthday one time. We had a pair of 'em for a while.'

Abrana turned from the rail and looked at him. 'I felt badly when Apolinaria told me of that,' she said. 'It was some years ago, but I remember it.'

'It's all right,' Clay said, and felt abashed, now, at having mentioned it. He had no business saying anything like that.

As though she understood his embarrassment, Abrana motioned with her arm toward the Morgan, which was frisking in the center of the corral, and laughed softly.

'He always seems so happy. Did Ygenio tell you he let me exercise your horse one morning? I hope you are not angry.'

'Angry?' Clay said. 'Why, no.' And as he thought of it he realized the idea didn't displease him, but rather, delighted him. Abrana Martinez would go very well upon the roan horse.

'That's all right,' he added. 'You ride him any time you want to. Would you like to now?'

Abrana smiled, her skin tight across her forehead, and her teeth white and even against her lips. 'I would like to very much, thank you; but I must go to Apolinaria now. I have kept her waiting long enough. Listen . . .'

And as though the girl's referring to the matter had evoked the summons, Apolinaria's voice called to her from the kitchen door.

'Abrana, *mie*; please to come, Abrana. There are the dishes.'

'You see?' Abrana's cheeks were round

with laughing. 'I already take too much time. Now I must go.'

'Yes,' Clay said. 'That Apolinaria's got a strong mind. You'll ride some other time?'

'Perhaps,' Abrana said.

The girl moved off and Clay considered joining her, and then thought better of it. Instead, he leaned against the corral pole and watched her walk through the sunlight toward the house. The light was hard and brilliant on her white blouse, and the contrast of her bare arms made them golden as she held them at her sides, with her elbows bent and her hands together at her waist. She was taking sturdy, light steps with her huarachos, like a boy would, and as she went across the gallery and through the door, Clay wondered why she was going back to White Oaks. Some time before she left he would have to ask Apolinaria about that.

4

In the early morning Clay had in mind to take his ride around the place. He wondered if Abrana would like to ride the red roan along with him, but after he had thought awhile he decided not to ask her. He wasn't sure of himself with her yet, and he knew he would be awkward. She didn't seem to be one with

39

whom he could be always casual and laughing, and he was afraid he might do something careless with her. He thought he'd better ride alone this time.

Ygenio came with him to the corral an hour after dawn to help him saddle up. Ygenio made a great thing of drawing up the cinch, nudging the roan's belly with his knee, and Clay got the notion he would like to come along. But since he had not asked Abrana, Clay wanted to do this thing alone; and he explained it that way to Ygenio.

'I just want to look around,' he said. 'I ain't had a ride over our land for I can't think how long, and I figure I better get used to it again.'

'All right, you go, Clay,' Ygenio said. 'You go and get it in your insides once more.'

'I won't be long,' Clay said. 'Anyway, I'll be back by noon.'

'All right. You take your time. Apolinaria will wait dinner for you.'

'I can live on what she gave me yesterday for quite a while,' Clay said. 'Don't bother 'bout me. You people go ahead.'

'Well, she will save something, then.'

'All right,' Clay said. 'That's fine. *Adiós.*'

Clay rode a long distance that morning. His land ran for many miles along the Pecos to the north and he intended to cover most of them. He was weary and aching still from the long haul down from Vegas, but this didn't bother him. He was riding across his own land and there was a point in it. He would never be too tired to do a thing like that.

Toward noon he had covered a share of it, and coming back, he stopped at last upon a rise a mile or so to the north of the buildings down below. From that point, he could see nearly everything that God had made in that great country. A man could stand up there and look and look until he felt no bigger than a grain of sand. He could look away out east and see the wide sky bending down to join the unbroken land in a fine, indefinite line. He could see the bronze scar the Pecos etched in the pallid earth and river meadows, and the faintly raised ridge of the Mescalero far beyond. He could see forever, and it was only the beginning.

And if seeing all that didn't make him feel humble and small and considerably less important than a lot of people thought they were, he could turn his head until he caught the dry wind from Arizona in his nose, and see the Capitans and Sacramentos rearing honest and eternal in the west. Their vast blue shoulders were cloaked in piñon, cedar, great spruce and groves of trembling aspens. Their crags and canyons held more secrets than one could ever hope to learn, and a man could only fill himself with a far-off lonesome emptiness when he wondered about them all.

Looking upon those shadowed islands, Clay felt this lonesome emptiness, and a portion of it remained with him as his eyes came around and passed along the slope to the clustered buildings underneath him in the trees. For some reason or other his mind had never ventured forward to the time when he'd have that place alone; when the responsibility of judgment would be his, and when no Hardin would be around to vex with questions and the like. They had built with an attitude of permanence in those early days, and Clay's young mind had been impressed with the notion that the older order could never end.

Seeing those buildings dozing in the sun, mottled here and there by the cottonwood shade, made him feel a little bit uneasy. He was glad to be home again, but seeing it all at once, as he was doing now, made him understand the size of the task he was figuring to undertake. It would be enough if everything was proper and in order, getting his hand in again, but with the help as Ygenio had explained it, and with dry rot and termites and whatnot getting ahead of maintenance, it could be the kind of uphill pull that might never find the crest.

It made him wonder if it wouldn't be the best thing to do as Ygenio had suggested. Dodge, or someone, would take it off his hands, if he was of a mind to leave.

He'd been up there looking around for twenty minutes or so when the horsemen came into the lane below and dismounted in the dooryard. He'd been up there, pondering his uncertain destiny and letting his eyes and thoughts roam about the land in which he stood. He was particularly looking at Dodge Liston's land, adjoining his own, and wondering what it was that made some men more hungry in the matter of range than others, when these riders came into the lane and stood down and stretched themselves in the fat shade of the trees.

He rode on down to find out who they were and what was on their minds, and he recognized them as he came around the corral and approached them on the roan horse. There were half a dozen of them and he thought how little they had changed since he had seen them last—the Gallagher brothers, Old Man Medford, Jack Harris, Dodge Liston; and one, he found on second look, that he didn't recognize. This one still remained upon his horse, and rolled a smoke in a somehow disinterested way, as though he was in attendance on these others simply because he had nothing better to do just then. But he held Clay's attention because Clay had not seen anyone wear a gun lashed down like that since he had run away from Robey Moore.

These men had an undecided air about them which gave Clay the notion that he was somehow in command of the situation. They had the appearance of men who had come upon a delicate mission and were not exactly certain in what way they were going to broach the matter. Each kept looking at the others, as though hoping someone else would get it going. Only the unknown, of all of them, seemed to know what he was about, and appeared not to give a damn for anything.

'Well,' Clay said after he stepped down, 'I don't expect you came out here just to admire one another's faces like that. What do you want?' He didn't feel hospitable.

Old Man Medford's wattles moved. 'Why, we came out here to welcome you home, Clay, just like good neighbors ought to do. I'm damned if that ain't why we came.'

'That's right,' Steve Gallagher said. 'We come out here to see how you was, and to see how you was doin' now that you got back from—from . . .'

Steve Gallagher looked like he had an unfamiliar tasting piece of food in his mouth and didn't know what to do with it. Clay smiled in a wry way and helped him out.

'Prison, Steve. That's where I got back from.'

He looked them over again, and gave the man on the horse a careful study. 'I don't think I know you very well,' he said.

'Name of Sam Chandler,' Dodge Liston said. 'He's helping out with the law around here for a spell.' Dodge Liston spoke with ease and his heavy face looked cool and dry in the heat of the day. His clothes were neat and well cared for and he seemed to get an assurance from knowing that. But Clay could remember when Dodge was no different from any other nester in the old days.

Clay let his eyes come around to the mounted man again. He had a feeling he was being estimated by this Chandler person. He'd seen men regard him in just that measuring way before and he was reminded somewhat of the impression that Billy the Kid had sometimes made. It made him think that Sam Chandler was like as not aware of that himself and no doubt derived a deal of pleasure from it. There were a lot of two-bit gun hands picking up Billy's mannerisms now that the Kid was dead.

'Howdy,' Clay said presently. 'You find good huntin' with all that firepower?'

'Not much yet,' Sam Chandler said. 'Never can tell what might pop up, though.'

'No, I don't suppose you can,' Clay said. 'Best to keep your eyes peeled.'

'I think that's a good idea,' Sam Chandler said. 'I thank you for it.'

'No need for that at all,' Clay said. 'Glad to oblige.'

Old Man Medford cleared his throat noisily. 'We come to explain that things around these parts have changed, Clay. We're a pretty law-conscious lot around here now, and we don't have no more shootin' or range wars or trouble of that sort.'

Clay measured Old Man Medford carefully. He remembered him as a sincere man, but a busybody, too, who was inclined to swing as the wind might blow.

'It's nice to learn that,' Clay said. 'Can't get much work done with all that kind of trouble goin' on. As you can see for yourself, my place here is pretty well run down because of the last one.'

'I was gettin' around to that,' Old Man Medford said. 'Maybe it's so run down and gone to seed and such that you was thinkin' of leaving it altogether. Could be you'd make out better somewhere else.'

Clay turned it over and picked up the slant of the conversation. Now he understood the purpose of the visit and it was clear to him that the others were relieved that everything was finally in the open. A big breath of air seemed to go out of all of them.

'That could be so,' he said into the silence. 'I guess I ain't been back long enough yet to give it much thought, though.'

'The Moore crowd's been hangin' around the country, Forrest,' Steve Gallagher said, 'and we don't like it one bit.'

'Can't say I blame you,' Clay said. 'You ought to get Pat Garret on their trail. I heard in prison he was pretty good at pickin' off the remnants of the fighters. He got Billy the Kid up at Pete Maxwell's place, as I remember. In a dark room, but he got him. Ain't Pat the cowman's sheriff any more?'

'Not since he done for Bonney and his pals,' Dodge Liston said. 'That's all he took the job for; just to get them and put an end to all their rampagin'. After the war was over, they couldn't seem to change their habits.'

'And there's others like 'em, still around.' It was Steve Gallagher again, and Clay looked at him.

'You can't seem to get that out of your head, can you, Steve?'

'We remember you was once a part of Moore's crowd,' Steve Gallagher said.

'In the fighting, I was,' Clay said. 'Before they went wholly outlaw. But that's done and I ain't with 'em no more. Pa was in that outfit, too. Come to think of it, Pa and me was among the few from hereabouts that got into that scrap at all. You might even say that Pa and me fought your battles for you at that time. I don't recall that I saw any of your faces up there on the Bonito or the Ruidoso.'

Old Man Medford took it up again. Old Man Medford had thick blue veins in the loose fat of his neck, and they bulged when he became excited. 'That ain't neither here nor there, Clay,' he said. 'That's all dead an' buried an' don't mean nothin' any more. We're just sayin' the Moore bunch is still in the country, and for all we know you may still have a fond remembrance for 'em.'

Clay leaned against the tie-rail and eyed Sam Chandler. Chandler had kept to himself in the talk-around, but as the temper of the meeting quickened his hands had drifted to his belt line, like he had trained himself for trouble. 'Maybe it's time you people took off,' Clay said. 'I had a hard morning, and I ain't much for talking just now.'

'Maybe you're something for thinking, then,' Steve Gallagher said. 'Might be good for you to do some of that.'

They mounted up and rode off, but Dodge Liston lingered on.

'You oughtn't to say things like that, Clay; they get ideas.'

'What'd I say, Dodge?'

'About Billy the Kid and Pat in the dark room. Like that.'

'It's true, ain't it? He done it at Fort Sumner; in Maxwell's bedroom. That's the way it come to me in prison.'

'There was no other way; he'd about paralyzed the country. Something had to give. The cattlemen knew Pat could do it if he could pin him down. That's why they put the job on him.'

'I know. It was bound to happen. I don't think one way or the other about it. If anything, I suppose I'm glad. I'm a cattleman, too, Dodge; I don't hold with outlawry. I'll side a man in a range-wide scrap, but does he go bad at the end of it, I'm against him.'

'I think that's what Medford and the boys were wondering about. Moore and his crowd are the last ones out. Everything's quiet but for them.'

'I'm no part of 'em, Dodge; put your mind at rest.'

Dodge looked up at the cottonwood limbs above, like he was seeking inspiration there, then down at Clay again.

'They mean business, Clay,' he said. 'There's a new situation in this valley. We're waking up down here. The whole of New Mexico's waking up, now that the fighting's ended. The Santa Fe's gone through to Albuquerque, and she's going straight on out to California. And we're going to have a railroad down here, too, one of these days. Speaking of Garret, he's even got him an idea 'bout bringin' in artesian wells; think of that for farming, Clay. This is gettin' to be civilized country, son. And the people living here, and coming out to settle, aim to make it that way. And to keep it so.'

'That's all very fine, and I'm in favor of it,' Clay said. Dodge was building up to something and he wondered what it was. Then he thought of the dark room again and Billy Bonney gurgling on the floor. Clay remembered him as dangerous and impulsive and he had never liked him. But still it would have been better in the open.

'That Lincoln County fighting was a foolish

49

business,' Dodge said of a sudden, off on a new thought.

'I suppose it looks that way to some,' Clay said. 'Folks didn't think so at the time.'

'Sure as hell never settled anything. Ain't none of 'em alive that started it. And of the ones that sided either way, them as ain't dead is ruined.'

'Look at Pa, huh, Dodge? Or me?'

'Well, now, I wasn't exactly thinking of you, but I guess you do come close to fitting in. But it's true, what I say; and look at Lincoln town. Less than five years ago it was a metropolis, and today it's sound asleep. And it ain't goin' to wake again, either.'

'I guess you got it figured out, all right, Dodge. I'd go again, though, and so would Pa.' Clay moved away from the rail and took a stance a few feet out.

'Now, tell me where you stand, Dodge. Seems to me you rode in here with Medford and the others.'

'I ain't maybe so hard as them, Clay. I rode in with 'em, all right, but it's different with me. If you was choosin' to leave I might be able to give you a decent price.'

'That's something worth considerin',' Clay said. 'What kind of price might that be?'

Dodge Liston ran his hand along his smoothly shaven face. 'Well, I'd have to figure some on that. 'Course, your place ain't near as good as it used to be, now, Clay. She's run

50

down pretty bad and I hear some of your beef wandered off while you was away. Them buildings, now, they'd need some attention; a lot of it. Might even be best to tear some down altogether and start new.'

Clay rocked on his heels and listened to it. It was almost a pleasure to hear a man carry on like that. Dodge never blowed hard and loud like Old Man Medford or the Gallaghers; he had no shout and bluster to him. He simply flowed along smooth and easy, and he was the more dangerous because of it.

'I don't suppose the possibility of the Santa Fe buildin' this way some time would make much difference, would it?' Clay said. 'That might even make this run-down no-account place a thing of value. But that wouldn't enter into your figurin', now, would it, Dodge?'

Dodge was in the shade, but his face was colored like the sun was shining on it anyway.

'I wouldn't know nothin' about what the Santa Fe might do,' he said. 'I'm just trying to do you a favor, is all.'

Dodge caught up the reins of his bridle, turned his stirrup and heaved himself into the saddle. He sat square and solid and as respectable as a preacher, looking down at Clay. 'I expect it'd do you some good to think it over.'

'I expect it would,' Clay said. 'And in the meantime, I'm goin' to get some help out here and put the place in shape.'

Dodge raked his fingers through the mane of his horse, and smiled. 'Kind of odd about that,' he said. 'All the spreads hereabouts has been hirin' like crazy lately. Ain't much good help to be found at any price.'

'Like that, huh?'

'Like that, Clay. *Adiós.*'

Dodge swung his horse around and headed down the cottonwood alley, and Clay stood there and watched the shadows of the branches make their curious patterns across his back. Some of them trees had been set out by Hardin, but others were as old as any man around there could recall. Their roots were deep and they held memories.

Ygenio came up from the corral as Dodge passed beyond the turn and out of sight.

'I watch you riding before, Clay,' he said. 'I see you standing on the rise back there and I wonder what you think. You maybe have it in your mind to leave this place?'

Clay stared down the cottonwood canyon, watching the old ghosts moving among the warted trunks. 'Yeah, I guess I did,' he said. 'I'm figurin' to stay on, though, after all. Them trees are sure pretty, ain't they?'

'*Si*,' Ygenio said. 'Yes, they are life itself.'

*　　　*　　　*

Apolinaria was making corn bread when Clay came inside to eat. The rest of them had already finished, but she had saved some frijoles and bacon for him, and the coffee pot bubbled on the stove in the cooking alcove. When he was seated at the table, she brought the food to him and poured the coffee; then continued with the corn bread as she talked to him.

'I am glad you come from your ride when you do, Clay,' she said. 'I see those *hombres* riding in and I think it will be *muy malo*. They are troublemakers, those.'

Clay spoke between mouthfuls of the frijoles and slow sips of the steaming coffee. 'Who, Dodge and Old Man Medford and that crowd? They don't know what trouble is. They just like to hear themselves talk.'

'No, they are for trouble, certain,' Apolinaria said. 'I know. They come before, when you are gone away. Sometimes one or two, sometimes three, maybe more. Always they want to know the same thing—when we expect you back again.'

'Well, now they know, so they won't be around to bother you any more,' Clay said.

'They will come again,' Apolinaria said quietly. She was very active with the bread, and her face was concealed from Clay. 'Now that you are here, they will try to drive you out again.'

'Fat chance,' Clay said. 'I'm here to stay and they know it. They just feel they got to make some kind of show of civic indignation, that's all. They made their gesture, and that's the end of it.'

'I am happy you are so certain,' Apolinaria said with faint sarcasm. 'They are bad, those men. Their hearts are hard and filled with greed.'

'Some of 'em are maybe that way,' Clay said. 'You see that one who stayed on his horse around here before? They call him Sam Chandler; he's new to me.'

Apolinaria thought before she answered. 'I see him one time. Maybe he comes more often, but I see him only one time. He comes with the Señor Liston. They come and ask for you, a month, maybe six weeks back.'

'With Dodge, huh? There's a sly one for you.'

Apolinaria did not have anything to add to that and she was quiet while Clay, who had finished eating, rolled and lit a cigarette. Except for the soft sounds Apolinaria made with the corn bread there was a warm and drowsy quiet over everything. The lack of sound in the house turned his mind to Abrana Martinez, for he was certain she was not inside; but Apolinaria anticipated him, and spoke of her.

'I send Abrana to clean the bunkhouse this afternoon,' she said. 'Since you will be bringing men in here to help, you will require it, and it is dirty like sin from lack of use. Does it annoy you that she comes to stay here while

54

you are gone?'

Clay took the cigarette from his mouth. 'Annoy me? Of course not. I'm glad she came. She can stay as long as she likes.'

'She will go soon,' Apolinaria said. 'She will return to White Oaks.'

Clay didn't wish to sound as personally interested as he was aware of feeling, and he approached it carefully. 'There's no need for that. There's room for everybody here. She don't have to go back there. Unless she's got someone to return to,' he added.

'She has no one any more; they are gone. But she will return there anyway.'

'Well, as she wishes, then,' Clay said, and he wondered if his studied unconcern was going over with Apolinaria. It was hard to make a point, yet not appear involved with it.

Apolinaria's bland face was turned toward him as she explained it further. 'It is not what Abrana wishes, Clay; it is I who want her to return. It is time for her to go soon.'

'Time?' Clay said. He didn't understand it. 'What do you mean by that?'

Apolinaria glanced through the window giving out on the dooryard, and inclined her head in that direction.

'Those, I mean,' she said. 'And the trouble they bring with them. I do not want Abrana to be a part of it.'

Clay laughed. 'I thought we had that settled. They won't do nothin'. They don't

55

want to start anything.'

Apolinaria shrugged and worked with the bread again.

'Perhaps, perhaps not. *Quién sabe?* But there are others. Now that you are here they will come again. They come before, too, as do the ones who come today, but it will be different now.'

'Who?' Clay said. He knew what she was talking about, but he was feeling tight inside, and he wanted her to say it.

'The old crowd you ride with before.' Apolinaria said it quietly.

'Robey, huh?' Clay ground his cigarette deliberately on the edge of the empty plate. 'I don't think he will.'

'Perhaps not. Perhaps he will not come at all, as you say, but I do not want Abrana to be a part of that. She has enough trouble in a natural way; she is very young and I do not want life to be brutal with her.'

Clay thought it over, toying with the coffee cup, making small rings of moisture on the table with the bottom of it. 'Maybe, if you think it's going to be that bad, you and Ygenio would want to leave, too.'

'I hope you intend a jest with what you say,' Apolinaria said. 'You should know that we will never leave this place until you leave as well. We are here together for more than fifteen years, and it is home to us. It is not kind of you to say such things.'

Clay felt deeply shamed, and he apologized. 'I didn't mean that,' he said. 'I'm sorry. I didn't mean anything by it; I just thought you might be worried.'

'Not for ourselves, but for Abrana. What happens to us here is willed by the *Dios*, because we are a part of it, but Abrana can avoid it. Do you understand it now?'

'Yes,' Clay said. 'I understand.'

He stood up from the table, feeling awkward and abashed. He wanted to discuss Abrana further, but Apolinaria had closed the matter, and he didn't wish to give offense to her by going on with it. He paused in the door, and with contrived lightness said, 'Well, don't toss her out right away. Give her a chance to finish up the bunkhouse.'

'Yes,' Apolinaria said. 'She will not leave that soon. She will finish it. I will decide when she is to go.'

5

They worked hard in those days and there never seemed an end to it. It made no difference what time of the early morning they rolled out; they were never finished with what they had to do when day was done. Sundown always found the work piled as high and endless as the day before, and it sometimes seemed that death itself would bring their only respite.

Ygenio was uncomplaining in the saddle, but he would agonize like a *penitente* in his *morada* when it came to work around the house and other buildings. He did not at all mind a saddle underneath him for endless hours, or even days, but when his fingers found themselves about a hammer handle or a saw he was apt to be smitten with fatigue and lassitude. He could not stand a thing like that for long, and he was always seeking causes to be sent out on the range again.

Clay knew he needed help, and badly. The two of them could hardly hope to get the place in shape and run it properly. There was too much of it that got beyond them; it required the greatest kind of effort from them both, and still it got ahead.

He took to riding into town to see what he could find. Only a few trips, though, and he came to know that it was about as Dodge had prophesied. Every able hand had long since signed with other outfits, or was elsewise occupied, and Clay wasn't of a mind to cull the bars and gambling joints for the dregs that might be found in them. One or two of that stripe mightn't go badly, if he could watch them all the time, but that was out, and he needed those who'd accept responsibility and do their work without an eye forever on their backs.

He got help in an unexpected manner. He came upon it in his own back yard. He had given up any hope of finding it in town, and he stayed pretty close to home. There was nothing to be found down there, and he didn't like the way the people in that town would look at him. They made him think of those evil-lookers up in Vegas. They made him think of Robey, and tended to keep his association with that man fresh and poignant in his mind. They would not let him forget he'd served prison time for murder.

So he stayed close to home.

He worked mostly around the buldings, but sometimes that would weary him and he would then ride out and breathe the dry wind moving over the sweep of grass that was his range. One day he walked the roan horse out beyond the rise to the north and when he crossed the crest and paused to look around he saw the rider working up the other side, coming in a long slant from the Pecos boundary of his land.

Clay backed off, swung down and pulled his lever-gun from the saddle scabbard. He lay behind a growth of yucca and watched this new one coming up the slope. He was coming slowly and taking his time and stopping every now and then to hike up in his stirrups and take a look around him. It didn't seem to Clay that he was simply passing through.

He was pretty close when he got down and

hunched along the slope to get an eye on the buildings on the other side. Clay could make him out as being young, boylike, almost, and see that he was humping up the rise in a manner that betokened wariness and a certain caution, as though he wasn't sure of what he was about. However, he'd left his rifle in the boot.

Clay waited for him to settle down before he moved. Then he slipped over the rise and worked down to where he could get behind the other. As he neared the horse he squatted quiet for a moment and studied it. The animal was a wiry little mustang with clean and hardy lines. It wore a plain, neat saddle with a minimum of decoration, and there was an air of competence about the other gear upon it. It made him think its rider might be a good hand when it came to handling beef. But the flank of that horse was etched with Old Man Medford's brand.

Clay edged up the slope directly to the rear of the man lying belly-down in the grass. When he got fifteen yards away he knew he'd been right about thinking him a youngster. The boy had removed his hat and was reclining with his chin upon his crossed arms out in front of him. There were big orange freckles on the one cheek that Clay could see, and his hair was a smash of rust upon his head. His gun was down along his hip and there wasn't much that he could do when Clay kneed up and took the rifle into both his hands.

'Howdy,' Clay said to him. 'You lookin' for someone?'

The young man turned around slow and careful, and put his hands up. 'Clay Forrest,' he said. 'Mister Clay Forrest.' It was a question and statement both.

'You got it right,' Clay said. 'What you doin' up here?'

'I'm just lookin', Mister Forrest, is all. I was just lookin' at your buildings down there. Little old Rusty Rhodes was just takin' a *pascar* over here to have a look.'

Clay felt a smile poking at the edge of his mouth, but he kept it out of sight. 'So, I see,' he said. 'I been watchin' you for fifteen minutes. Seems to me you could have been more careful.'

'Sure I could, but I didn't come to do no harm,' Rusty Rhodes said.

'You're another one I ain't seen around before,' Clay said to him. 'New, are you?'

'Ain't been here but a few years. Came on this way after my ma got took by fever in Abilene. Never did have no pa that I know of. Real name's Dunston. Too fancy so they just call me Rusty. I'm on my own, have been since I was fifteen.'

'Kind of a maverick, ain't you?' Clay said.

'Could say that, I guess. I know how to work, though. I been on my own long enough to learn. Just now lookin' at your spread down there; I figure I could put my hand to shorin' up them saggin' corners, square up them old shingles, an' mend them fences proper.'

A part of Clay's smile moved the corner of his lips up. 'That horse of yours is wearin' Old Man Medford's brand.'

'I know,' Rusty said. 'And I'm goin' to miss him. Ain't many can stick with a steer like him. Almost dogs 'em down by hisself.'

'Ain't you happy with Old Man Medford?'

'I don't guess I am. I ain't set on the way they like to talk over there. I came over here to see if you was as bad as some of them make you out. Don't seem you could be, but I had to be sure.'

Clay put the rifle in his lap when he sat down. Rusty Rhodes's wide face split clear across in its smile, and he rubbed his arms as he let them down.

'I ain't so bad,' Clay said. 'They just figure 'cause me and Pa fought in the war that we is a smirch on the fair name of this valley. We had a notion that we was doin' right, though.'

'Uh huh,' Rusty Rhodes said. 'I was pretty young then, but I remember some of it. I was only a kid, though, and couldn't get into it.'

Clay worked up a cigarette and lit it. 'How did you feel about that business?'

'I felt a little sorry to hear about that John Tunstall gettin' killed that way.' Rusty Rhodes took a sidewise look at Clay as though he was checking for reaction.

'I guess we'd of seen eye to eye on it, then,' Clay said. 'You'd of been unpopular with some, though.'

'I already worked that out,' Rusty Rhodes said. 'Most I know said it was bad to take sides in a big thing like that, with hired gunmen comin' in an' all. They said only fools'd ride into that.'

'I remember such talk at the time,' Clay said.

'I guess maybe that's why I got curious about you,' Rusty Rhodes said. 'That's why I come up to have a look at your place when I heard you was back. Given time, I might even have got the nerve to come and rap on your door.'

'You figure you're satisfied now?'

'Nope. I reckon I'm still curious.'

'This can likely shape up into something big,' Clay said. 'I already had all kinds of invitations to leave again.'

'I know about that, too. It don't make no difference.'

Clay stood up and squashed the shuck beneath his boot heel. 'I guess we'd better get down below, then. Bring your horse and we'll get him back to Medford somehow. We got some pretty fair ones on our string.'

'All right. I'd like to keep him, but I don't guess that's the best thing, is it?'

'No, I don't guess it is. Ain't no sense in

63

breedin' trouble. You know this Sam Chandler?'

'I know of him. They got him to work up here for the stockmen's group. I guess he works for everybody. They say he's handy, but I can't say from experience.'

'They ain't tryin' to fit him into Garret's boots, are they? He don't look like quite the size.'

'No, it ain't nothin' like that. He's strictly on the stock-group payroll. He ain't workin' for the County any.'

'Uh huh,' Clay said. 'Well, we learn a little each day.'

They walked on down the slope to get Rusty's horse, then went back up on the long slant toward the roan. Driving his legs into the incline made Clay aware of the gnawing in his belly, and he remembered he hadn't eaten in several hours.

'Say,' he said to Rusty Rhodes as the new thought came to him of a sudden, 'you hungry?'

'I surely am,' Rusty said. 'Seems I ain't et nothin' in a week. I guess that skulkin' in the grass gets a feller's appetite up.'

They came across the crest and Clay was laughing softly. 'Apolinaria's goin' to like this,' he said. 'This is goin' to be a holiday for her.'

*　　　*　　　*

Rusty Rhodes was a hard and able worker. He was clever with tools, and he had a good, strong back for lifting. These qualities endeared him greatly to Ygenio, and his appetite was continuing delight to Apolinaria. He fit into things pretty well around the place, and they began to get things done.

But it was not all work. If the days were long and strenuous, the evenings were the more relaxing and enjoyable because of it. When they were through with eating they would gather on the gallery, and they would all be fine and laughing with one another. Sometimes, in the coolness, they would build a fire in the dooryard, and sit around and crack piñons by the light of it. Other times, Ygenio would play upon his old guitar and sing the half-forgotten songs and ballads in the ancient Spanish idiom of that country. A person was inclined to lose himself in the wanderings of those melodies, and forget entirely that Ygenio's voice was coarse and broken, so great a charm did he exert.

Less frequently, for she was shy, Abrana Martinez would dance for them. It was always necessary for Apolinaria and Ygenio to set the mood for this; and while Rusty would play for them they would bounce with clumsiness about the dooryard in a *jota*, or perhaps an old folk dance which had no sort of name at all. When they collapsed, perspiring and roaring, upon the gallery, they would prevail upon

Abrana; and Ygenio would play for her.

'A fandango, Abrana, *mio!*' they would gasp. 'A fandango!'

Clay was very conscious of her at these times. Now and then she would accompany her dancing with a pair of castanets, and other times Ygenio would provide the music by himself. Either way, it made no difference to Clay, for when she commenced to dance he was seldom aware of the music anyway. He would only sense it as a background against which Abrana would cast her movements, her golden legs flashing as they reflected the burning of the piñon logs, her huarachos skittering like dry leaves before the wind, her blouse pressed thinly against the contours of her body, her hair springing outward like a mane, and her eyes wide and wild with black fire.

On such occasions Clay might experience a suffocating sensation in his chest and find a strange pulse beating in his throat. He would sometimes catch Ygenio regarding him with amusement as he played the music, or Apolinaria with a more thoughtful speculation, and he would wonder what there was about himself that seemed so obvious. It would incline him to be very careful in the way he acted. It made him feel foolish to behave this way, but he couldn't help himself.

One evening a hiatus developed in the after-supper routine; Apolinaria discovered she had sewing to be done, and Ygenio disclosed a longing for a good night's sleep. Rusty Rhodes remained on the gallery with Clay and Abrana for a time, en-gaging in desultory conversation, until he recalled that he'd intended to mend a lariat, and he departed to look into this.

Alone with Abrana by the piñon fire, Clay felt a sudden clumsiness. It was one thing to talk horses with her in the open sunlight, but quite another to be sitting with her by the firelight in the dooryard. In the one he was on firm ground, the acknowledged and undisputed master, but in this other he felt that God or nature had endowed women with a natural superiority. In the firelight she had a complicated aspect of depth and mystery.

In desperation, he suggested a walk down the cottonwood lane. 'Have you ever seen the lights from the end of it?' he said.

'I do not think so,' Abrana said. 'What lights are there to see?'

'Those in the village,' Clay said. 'You can always see them good from up here.' He felt slightly foolish discussing the lights that way.

'All right,' Abrana said. 'I would like to see them. Lights are always pretty from far off at night.'

'Yes,' Clay said. He took her arm to assist her from the gallery, and it was warm and round beneath his hand. They went across the dooryard and into the darkness of the trees,

67

and she did not attempt to take her arm away. He had his hand held underneath, and his fingers lay along her wrist. They walked quietly with no talk between them, but he could feel the warmth of her, and the life running through her wrist.

When they came to the open place at the end of the alley she stepped away from him and watched the lights. He stood behind her and saw her head a dark shadow against the sky, blotting out the stars.

'They are very beautiful,' Abrana said. 'It makes one wonder what all the people are doing down there.'

'You can see the town growing by those lights,' Clay said. 'Every now and then there's a couple new ones, and then you know a few more folks are taking up down there. They're comin' in pretty fast now; even faster'n Lincoln in the old days.'

Abrana moved to step onto a large rock, but Clay reached out and took her arm. He was undecided and half in doubt, until he turned her around and kissed her on the lips. She did not resist and her mouth was soft and smooth against his own. He felt nothing except her being warm against him, everywhere; and the blood pulse beating in his throat and head.

When she stood away from him, she turned to watch the lights again. Clay stood behind her, not saying anything. He was sure about her now, and he didn't want to make any mistakes with her.

'It is not good to do this.' She spoke to him in a small voice and continued looking at the lights.

'Why not?' he said. 'What's the matter with it?'

'It is not good. I am going soon, and it is not good to start something like this.'

'You don't have to go,' Clay said. 'There's no reason to.'

'It is not for me to say,' Abrana said. 'Apolinaria decides.'

'She doesn't have to,' Clay said. He was feeling impatient with the idea of Apolinaria running things. 'You can decide for yourself.'

They were walking toward the dooryard now. He held her arm again and their hands were clasped very lightly together. She walked close to him, but impersonally, like the hand clasp, not with pressure. They were still having the trouble with Apolinaria.

'No,' Abrana said. 'It is for her to say. I will go because I do not wish to give her anxiety.'

'She doesn't know,' Clay said. 'She just imagines. She is always imagining. Nothing will happen.'

'Even so, I cannot make her anxious. She is very good to me and I do not wish to worry her. I am not afraid for myself, but she is right; there will be trouble now. Apolinaria knows, and so does Ygenio. They know.'

Clay put pressure on her arm to stop her. He put his hands behind her shoulders and kissed her, and she slowly took his face in her hands and kissed him back, hard at first, then soft. Then she moved her arms up and they came smooth and tight against his neck. When she removed them she did not look at him again, but turned away and walked swiftly across the dooryard to the house. Clay stood watching her until the door closed; then he went to the dying fire and began to pour sand on the spitting embers. The piñon smoke had a rich smell to it in the night.

6

Much of the time Rusty stayed around the ranch in those first days of his residence. He put his hand to splitting new cedar shingles for the roof of the house, and for those of some of the other buildings. With straw and watered hardpan, he mixed adobe in the Spanish fashion, and chinked the many cracks and seams that time and weather had created in the timbers. With an old bucksaw, he cut new poles to replace the worst of those that had cracked and splintered in the corral. And he used an adz and a latent artistry to hew and form new *vigas* for those buildings whose roofs were not pitched and shingled and were in danger of collapsing.

Sometimes Rusty would have to take the wagon to the hills to get the timber for these projects. A good deal of scrap material had accumulated around the place from building in the past, but Rusty was sometimes fussy and he would then despair of anything he hadn't cut for himself. So he would take the wagon to the hills for pine and cedar.

One day he set out to do this in the early morning. The sun had come above the Mescalero in the east, and the land lay bronzed and golden in the quiet light. The trees and grass stirred imperceptibly in the sleepy air, which though still and warm possessed a shining clarity and did not seem quite in character with the apparent drowsiness. Across the curve of sky the tawny shading, imparted by the light, deepened into azure and more subtle gradations until, in the far west, the sun-emblazoned peaks appeared to rear from shoulders deep in purple.

It was a time of day that belonged to the birds and animals. After helping Rusty with the hitching, Clay stood in the doorway of the feed barn, watching him depart, and he was conscious of the wild life stirring all around him, and about the wagon creaking forward. It was an hour when the sounds those creatures made carried great distances, and their activity seemed to dominate all existence.

A magpie quarreled with Rusty's off-horse,

imparting loud vituperation at his disturbance of the morning calm. Startled in their turn by the magpie's excitement, a covey of quail lifted in a flurry and departed, their small and compact bodies blurred in flight. A jack rabbit bounded off in reaching strides. And far away, so far, indeed, that Clay could only guess at its position, a coyote sang a morning song, and Clay wondered idly if that portended rain, as Ygenio would be sure to hold. Some yards away from him, a vine garroon stretched its many legs and sunned itself. Clay felt at peace, and momentarily contented.

The spell of this endured until Rusty had the wagon out of hearing, and only then did Clay stir from his unintended indolence. He was aware that he had spent a good deal more time in idle admiration of the day than he likely should have, and he set about the jobs at hand with a lurking sense of guilt. It was all very well to marvel at the full curve of a cloud ship sailing on the upper winds, or to seek the meaning of a blue-jay's scolding, but such pursuits had never been known to turn a dollar anywhere.

He got to work. He had intended to join Ygenio in a casual counting of the calves, but in recent days the well pump's squeal had become a shriek, and Apolinaria had been beside herself because of it. So Clay went to work on this disturbance.

It was a quiet undertaking, which did not

require concentration, and still bemused, he was receptive to the sounds of activity reaching out to him. The insects buzzed and chittered in the hollyhocks and morning-glories which thrived against the building walls. Away somewhere, a white-faced Hereford bellowed in annoyance, or just to pass the time of day. Near by, the sound of running hooves told of playfulness among the corralled remuda. And in the intervals of silence which spaced these other sounds, he'd hear the laughter, chatter, and sometimes quiet singing, of Abrana and Apolinaria as they went about their business in the house.

One time Apolinaria came to the kitchen door and looked at him in such a way that made him think she might have something to discuss with him; but just then Ygenio came in upon his horse, and a moment later Rusty's team and wagon lurched and thundered toward them from the west.

Rusty's posture half-standing in the box, his feet braced and the brim of his hat a fan across his head—made Clay stand up and stare at him. Rusty swung the team in a braking arc around the feed barn, disappeared behind it, then appeared again and came to a thrashing halt as Ygenio grasped the bridles of the horses. By the time Clay dropped his tools and joined them, Rusty was already on the ground.

'You bounced all your timber out,' Clay said

73

when he came up. 'The Apaches jump the reservation?'

Rusty's freckled face was layered in dust and streaked with sweat, and Ygenio was laughing at him. 'I think he has a *bruja* after him. He comes like one who is pursued by many of those *brujas*.'

Rusty rubbed his sleeve across his eyes and got his breath. 'Witches, hell. And that goes for Apaches, too. And I didn't get near the timber neither. I come back to tell you about the tracks I found.'

Clay stood quietly, watching him. 'What tracks?'

'Tracks of the *brujas*, certainly,' Ygenio said. 'What else?' Ygenio was going to play it out.

'Cattle tracks, that's what,' Rusty Rhodes said. 'A couple, maybe three miles, over west. I didn't know we had anything over that way, so I come back to make sure.'

'We don't that I know of,' Clay said. 'Everything ought to be at the river. What about that, Ygenio? You just come back.'

'No,' Ygenio said, 'they are at the river. I did not count them, but they look the same as ever. How many of these tracks do you see, Rusty?'

'Twenty—maybe thirty—head, it looked like,' Rusty said. He straightened the brim of his hat. 'And looked like there was horses with 'em.'

74

Clay was conscious of spreading his legs for a better stance, and lifting his hands to his hips.

'They are not ours, then,' Ygenio said. 'I would know if thirty head were gone.'

'Horses,' Clay said. 'Which way was this parade going?'

'I didn't follow 'em none either way,' Rusty said. 'The tracks looked a couple days old. They come from the north down that barranca over there, then come up again at the south end of it and headed west. Looked like they was in it all the time.' Clay was thinking it out. In his mind he could see the area they were speaking of and he remembered how the barranca indented the earth and ran for many miles.

'If they was in it all the time it don't sound like any of our stuff. It might be they was brought through our place from somewhere else, just to get 'em out. That barranca's a mighty handy thing for something like that. We better have a look, though, just to make sure.'

'That's what I figured, too,' Rusty said. 'So I come back to shake this wagon.'

'All right, then,' Clay said. 'We'll get goin'. Will you saddle up, Ygenio? I got to put them tools away.'

'All right,' Ygenio said, and he spoke to Rusty as Clay turned away. 'You take my horse and go ahead if you wish. I will follow

75

with Clay.'

'Thanks,' Rusty said, and the sound of his mounting up and riding off carried to Clay as he walked back to the pump. The hooves were already pounding in a gallop, and the thought of Rusty's fooferaw made him want to laugh. Rusty sure was funny when he got excited, he was thinking. Damned near worth the price of whatever was out that way just to see him get like that.

*   *   *

Apolinaria was working the handle of the pump when Clay returned to get the tools. She moved it in experimental strokes, with her head bent slightly, carefully attentive for the old squeal.

'It's all right now,' Clay said to her. 'You won't have that any more. I fixed it.'

'It was very bad before,' Apolinaria said. 'I want to make certain it is gone. It cried like a lost soul.'

'Well, it's gone now. I cut some new leather for the plunger, and I oiled it some, too. If it comes back again you just pour a little water in it like you do for priming. It'll go away, then.'

'Yes,' Apolinaria said. 'I will do that.'

Apolinaria's hand remained on the handle, but it was dormant now. Clay was looking across her head, wondering where Abrana was, and he could feel the older woman's eyes exploring his face. It made him uneasy to know that she was doing this, and it occurred to him that she had not come out there simply to discuss the pump with him.

'Clay, you should not do that,' she said quietly, and then he looked at her. Her square-round face was upturned toward his, and there was an expression of concern in it which was disturbing.

'Do what?' he said. 'What did I do?'

'Play with Abrana the way you do. In the evening like you do. It is wrong.'

Clay felt a dull heat coming into his face. For a moment he could think of nothing.

'I wasn't playing with her,' he said then. 'We just went out to see the lights. We didn't do anything. Anything wrong.'

'I do not mean that. I mean there is danger and now you may do things which you do not mean and which later you will regret. Because they will be of no consequence then.'

'I don't think that way,' Clay said. 'I think you're all wrong about this danger in the first place, but even so, I wouldn't act like that. I wouldn't stampede.'

'No, of course not. But I am thinking of Abrana. Now that you have done this she will have anxiety for you. I can tell simply by looking at her. No matter what she would say if I should ask her.'

'My God,' Clay said. 'Is that all you people

do? Just go around bein' worried about each other? My God.'

And then he stopped. The shot came clean and sharp from far away and put a period to his exasperation. It was over beyond the buildings somewhere, in the general direction that Rusty had taken, and he thought, 'My God, now what?'

He turned around and ran. He was running toward the corral and thinking that Ygenio should have the horses ready now, and that he had the rifle somewhere with the saddle gear in the shed beyond the feed barn, and that something bad was surely happening out there. He was thinking all this and not trying to work any of it out, when he saw Ygenio coming out of the shed with the rifle, levering a cartridge.

Then he came around a shaggy screen of bushes and saw Rusty coming slowly down the curving rise, mounted up, with another person walking out in front of him, fastened on the muzzle end of Rusty's rifle barrel. This person was walking like that and Rusty was leading the other's horse behind his own. They were still far off, but Clay recognized the stranger anyway.

Only one man had a shambling, sidewinding walk like that. It was Diamond-Back, right-hand man for Robey Moore.

It was Rusty's show and Clay and Ygenio stood there watching him herd Diamond-Back into the dooryard before they got into it themselves. It was amusing to witness Diamond-Back's discomfort. Diamond-Back was not accustomed to walking for great distances, and Clay could tell he wasn't taking kindly to the treatment. His lean and hungry face was sullen and his long arms flapped belligerently at his sides. He was in a sour mood and Clay's laughter didn't seem to improve it any.

'Well, what'd you expect?' Clay said to him when Rusty had him standing in the middle of them. 'Can't nobody come prowling around without they're goin' to draw attention.'

'I was doing nothing whatsoever,' Diamond-Back said. 'I was simply comin' peaceful-like to see you, when this half-growed punk like to cut me down.'

This gave Rusty a laugh and he poked his rifle out and nudged Diamond-Back between the shoulders. 'He was up on the high ground out there, Clay. Funny thing, I was headin' for the barranca and I just did happen to glance over that way an' I seen this horse nuzzlin' at the grass. Then I spotted this feller sneakin' through it with his rifle, just like a snake. I thought best to shoot that out of reach and talk about it later.'

'I was just lookin' to see if it was clear, is all,' Diamond-Back said.

Clay rocked on his heels and eyed the outlaw. He was wondering if he appeared more menacing and unkempt than he had before; then decided that nothing but a bullet would ever make an appreciable change in a man like him.

'That's where he gets his name,' Clay said to Rusty. 'Kind of a snakelike feller, at that, when you come to think of it. Ain't many thievin', mean things he ain't done.'

Diamond-Back glared around him. Diamond-Back's face was sallow and bony and his features, no matter what his mood might be, always seemed to Clay to set themselves in an attitude of brutality. He was a carnivore who never ceased his hunting, and who never relaxed the caution of the hunted.

'Pretty smart-talkin', ain't you?' Diamond-Back was saying now. 'I seen the day when you wasn't so wise. I seen the day when you didn't know your right hand from your left.'

'I expect you did,' Clay said. 'Most everybody grows up and learns, though. Except for some. Them's the sort that generally comes in at gun point. Or goes under, depending on how they'll have it.'

Diamond-Back spat in the dry dust at his feet, the spittle rolling into little balls like buckshot. 'Talk's cheap, Forrest. Don't cost nothin' when you got the high hand.'

Clay fished the paper and tobacco from his pocket. He poured some for himself, then passed the stuff around. Everyone but Diamond-Back built up one.

'Don't smoke no more?' Clay asked him. 'Or are you choosy?'

'About the company, I am.'

'Never knew your pride would hold you from gettin' something you didn't have to pay for,' Clay said. Clay lit up and threw the match away. 'All right, now, you been runnin' beef from around here?'

'I wouldn't say if I had.'

'We got strong limbs on these trees here. I expect you could dance a brisk jig under one of them.'

'That wouldn't get you nowhere. I don't give a damn for that, and you ought to know it. We rode together.'

'Maybe you'll say what you're doin' here, then; you got a reason for slinkin' around up there.'

'Robey wants you back,' Diamond-Back said, and he got his assurance back. He appeared to take strength and swagger from the mention of that name. He pushed his thumbs in his belt and smiled around. 'He says you better get humpin' for the hills; he's been expectin' you for some time now. You made him unhappy by not showin' soon's you got out. That's why he sent me down.'

'He did, huh? I guess he's goin' to remain unhappy then. And you can tell him that. I already explained my stand to him one time before, but maybe he's forgotten. Or maybe he didn't think I meant it.'

'There ain't nobody leaves Robey permanent without his say-so, or without they're dead. You don't fit neither one of them descriptions yet.'

'Well, I did quit him, and you might refresh him on that point. Granted I done it the hard way, I still done it, and I ain't backtrackin'. He's got no complaint on me. I stuck with him through a good share of the scrapping, but I don't put up with that other business. I ain't no wanton killer.'

Diamond-Back worked up another smile. 'I heard a jury say different a few years back.'

'Juries have been wrong before, an' likely will be again. I killed no one; that was someone else's work, and I just happened to be handy to pin it on, but that's beside the point. I ain't comin' back to Robey and you can tell him for me personal. If he wants to go into it further he can come down here himself. Now you can go.'

'I ain't in no particular hurry,' Diamond-Back said.

'Think again,' Rusty Rhodes said, and he rammed the rifle into the outlaw's back again, hard. 'You heard the boss. Get on this animal.'

Diamond-Back's face got red and ugly, but he complied. He swung on up and sat in a mean hunk, glaring hard at Rusty. 'I got a good mind for faces, kid. I'll remember yours.'

'I got a nose for smells, myself,' Rusty said. 'I'll know when you're around.'

'All right, now—git.' Clay stepped to the side, swung his arm back and brought the dust leaping from the hide of the outlaw's horse with the flat of his hand, and the horse surged, startled. It ran ahead for five yards before Diamond-Back got it under hand, and the gun hand kept it moving out. He was heading into the grassland before anybody spoke again.

'I seen that brand,' Rusty Rhodes said into the quiet. 'It's Dodge Liston's. And he come right over here with it.'

'Yeah, Diamond-Back don't give a damn for nothin',' Clay said. 'That's a good joke on Dodge, though.'

'Do you think it is he who takes the cattle through the barranca?' Ygenio said easily.

'Maybe,' Clay said. 'Likely had a hand in it. I guess Old Man Medford had it straight. Robey's startin' to work this valley, all right, and I'm wonderin' why. We'll likely hear about what went through the barranca later on.'

A small polished stone lay at Clay's feet, and he stooped and picked it up. It felt clean and soft when he rolled it in his fingers, and somehow put him in mind of the smoothness of the early hours of the day.

Before all this had happened, he thought— and he threw the stone with viciousness. Before that snake-eyed sonofabitch had come and spoiled it all.

7

For some time after that Clay could not get Diamond-Back out of his head. Diamond-Back was in his mind like the remembrance of one of those old ballads which Ygenio would sometimes sing in the evening firelight, or like the soft and vivid turn of Abrana's body when she would dance. Like these, Diamond-Back would haunt his thinking for days on end and wouldn't leave for anything. Coming back home to this valley, he'd thought he'd had all those recollections disciplined and put away in their proper places in his memory, but now he found he hadn't.

Diamond-Back stayed back in there and watched him, his cold, unfeeling eyes unblinking in his lean and hungry face. Diamond-Back, and yes, those others whose living ghosts were once again evoked for his examination; Robey Moore and Ed Picket, Bob Fergus and Steve Howard, the lot of them. The term in prison had made them seem another lifetime and a million miles away, but Diamond-Back's appearance had changed it all again. He had restored to life those men of evil genius, and they were now as near and close to Clay as they had been at any time in the bloody and chaotic past. They were just over yonder, there, watching him;

watching him, and waiting for a chance to devil him.

Altogether, Clay rode with Robey's bunch for the best part of three months, beginning with the week of Hardin's killing, and ending with the battle at Blazer's Mill. They lived mostly in the hills and canyons and timber up around Lincoln, along the Bonito or the Ruidoso. When the weather was all right they camped out in the open, but sometimes they'd hole up at a place that belonged to friends, in isolated or forgotten cabins, old mine workings, and the like. Now and then they'd spend time in a kind of barracks McSween had rigged up in the store building he and Tunstall owned in Lincoln.

They were outdoor men, though, and it was better in the hills and forests. Even in the early spring when the weather was apt to be erratic, and the wind had the tearing edge of a dull knife, it was better outdoors than in that building of McSween's. And after Brady, Murphy's sheriff, had been gunned by Frank McNab and those who set the ambush with him, the streets of Lincoln were risky ground for the anti-Murphy forces anyway. So there was a point in keeping out of there.

The timber and the slow, blue hills around there were nice for Clay, though they seemed possessed of a greater drama than those he very dimly remembered in Missouri. They seemed to go on forever with not even a thought of ending, and every time he'd come around another bend there'd be a new lofty, battered crown to look upon. A man could marvel at the moods those hills took upon themselves, and though he looked forever he'd never see the same one twice. It was kind of terrifying to consider his own significance in the shadows of those lifting shoulders; but kind of restful, too. A man never doubted where he stood when he was up in there.

But they were partly spoiled for him when the day came for killing Buckshot Roberts. It was like he'd started in to take a part in some kind of dirty thing and the taint of it lingered in the timber after that. He'd known death and killing up in there before and he'd accepted it because that was a part of it, and was going to keep on being so until everything was ended.

But the Buckshot Roberts thing was different. When that happened the Lincoln fight became a bad taste in the mouth for him. More than anything, it impressed on him the fact that Robey was in it simply for the pleasure he derived from killing, and for the money to be had. It caused him to realize that he'd stayed on with Robey's crowd too long. It was the thing which finally drove him to make his break—God only knew why he hadn't made a getaway before. He'd followed Hardin's admonitions as fast as his conscience would let him go.

*   *   *

Nobody seemed to know just why they were
going up there to Blazer's Mill that day to
meet Dick Brewer, who'd been Tunstall's
foreman. If Robey knew the whole of it he
kept it to himself and the rest of them had
learned that it didn't always pay to bother
Moore with questions. They had gotten used
to being ruled with iron.

'Brewer's got himself a special constable's
badge somehow, an' we're goin' to meet his
posse up at Blazer's Mill,' was about all that
Robey said and he left it at that. The rest of
them could only wonder about it as they rode
along.

'Maybe Murphy's got him a big bunch
together up there and Robey and Brewer got
wind of it,' Ed Picket said.

'What business would Murphy have at
Blazer's?' Clay asked. 'The Indian Agency's
on that land; it's government property. It
don't seem sensible he'd risk a fight of any
kind up there.'

'Maybe there ain't goin' to be no fight,'
Steve Howard said. 'If Brewer's got him a
badge he maybe don't figure on nothin'
violent.'

'Everybody's got a badge when they want
one,' Clay said. 'It don't make no difference
what side they're on. Everybody figures what

87

he's doin' is right and just and lily pure, an' likes to have some sign of it. So he gets himself a badge somewhere, or a warrant, maybe.'

Steve Howard regarded Clay in a careful kind of way. Momentarily, it seemed that he might question this as heresy, but then he simply shrugged.

'Well, anyway, we don't know nothin',' he said. 'Likely ain't goin' to be no fight at all.'

'I didn't say there was goin' to be any fight,' Clay said. 'I just said it don't seem like good sense for Murphy to make trouble on that ground. Likely he'd be mixin' a real fracas then. He might even get himself a chase from the Stanton troopers, even though he is supposed to stand in good with 'em.'

Diamond-Back came up beside them in a widening of the trail. Robey's lieutenant always rode a piebald horse in those days and it made curious, grunting noises as it walked along. You always knew when Diamond-Back was near at hand.

'Feller named Buckshot Roberts hangs around up in there sometimes,' he said. 'He's got him a shack and a handful of stock in the valley, an' it's my guess this look-see has got to do with him.'

Clay turned it over in his mind and thought about it. It was a name he'd heard but a few times and he didn't connect it with any fighting in the past. He'd heard Roberts to be a homely old man who simply liked to live and let live, and that was all.

'Who's he?' he asked Diamond-Back. 'What's he got to do with all this?'

Diamond-Back hitched around in the saddle and smiled into the screen of juniper along the trail.

'Just an old goat who figures he don't have to take sides in this business. He ain't yet learned he can't stay neutral.'

'How come Brewer expects to arrest him for that?' Clay said. 'That's his own business, ain't it? That ain't no crime.'

'Depends on how you look at it,' Diamond-Back said. 'This Roberts feller is an old Indian-fighter. He's got enough lead in him to start his own shot foundry. They say he scarce can lift his arms for the dead weight of 'em. He's settin' a bad example.'

'How so is that?' Clay said. 'Don't sound to me like he could fight even did he want to. What's wrong with his stayin' out of it? A bunch is lucky simply not to have him draggin' at their heels; he wouldn't be no help.'

'He's loud,' Diamond-Back said. 'Fellers say he makes too much talk that don't sound right.'

'And Brewer thinks he can arrest him for a thing like that?' Clay said. 'That don't make sense.'

'Maybe Brewer ain't goin' to arrest him,' Diamond-Back said; and then he shrugged and looked away again. And that seemed to put an end to it.

They kept on riding. Clay rode close behind Robey and he kept his eyes on him. Robey surely sat his horse like a top-hand, and was thinking. Lots of fellers were pretty good at that, but like as not they left the impression of being conscious of what they were about; but not Robey. He rode like his horse was a part of him. Like it was maybe an arm or a leg that would do exactly what he'd planned for it to do without any real thinking on it, or guiding of it. But that was the way that he did everything. Like he knew far in advance exactly what was going to happen, and had already put his mind ahead to something else.

Buckshot Roberts stayed in Clay's mind. 'You don't figure all those people are goin' up there just to scrap it out with one old cripple, do you?' he asked Diamond-Back after a while.

'I don't know nothin',' Diamond-Back said. 'And I ain't botherin' my head about it. But what if we do?'

It was too important to Clay to let it rest with that, and he pushed the roan horse up to range with Robey Moore. Robey had his empty eyes off in the brush somewhere and it was a minute or so before he seemed to be aware of Clay.

'There's talk we're goin' up to Blazer's to see about an old cripple,' Clay said. 'This

Buckshot Roberts that don't choose to side with no one.'

When Robey looked at a man long and still that man got the notion he was naked and there wasn't nothing he could hide. Clay felt it that way now, and he picked at a seam in his pants so he wouldn't show it.

'Fellers ain't happy 'less they talk,' Robey said. 'And the less they know the more they got to say. I reckon that's human nature, but it surely is a stupid way to go about things.'

'Well, is it true or ain't it?' Clay said. 'Don't seem right to trouble a guy like that simply 'cause he's got his mind set in a way that don't please everyone else.'

'Well, you don't want to trouble your head about any trouble he might have,' Robey said. 'You was comin' along pretty well, and now you get nosy again. I thought we understood one another.'

'Why, I reckon we do,' Clay said. 'But this is something I figure I got a right to know about. I don't know yet whether I hold with this or not. Might be all right for Brewer to take him in, if'n he'll go, but he don't sound to me like the sort that will. That means fightin', and I ain't about to throw down on no old half-man like he must be.'

Robey took a long time thinking that one over. It seemed to Clay that he might never speak again before he said, 'You ain't, huh? Well.'

91

Clay knew they'd reached some kind of impasse, but he'd found his ground and he was standing on it. He'd never done a thing to be ashamed of in his life and he wasn't going to start under this man's teaching.

'No, I ain't,' he said; and he looked straight at Robey when he said it.

*   *   *

He saw the beginning of it when they came through the trees and approached Doc Blazer's mill on the Tularosa River. He saw this old, unkempt, defiant guy, who must be Buckshot Roberts, standing in a doorway and making talk with the riders already drawn up there in the open space before the building. Roberts held a rifle loosely in his hands as though he maybe had an intimation of what was going to happen. There were hard men in that company and their intentions were not artfully concealed.

Clay saw Buckshot Roberts making wary conversation with Dick Brewer. Dick Brewer's new authority was shining in the sun upon his vest. Besides Brewer there were ten or a dozen other men; mostly men that Clay knew, had seen around before, and there were some with whom he'd basked about a campfire, or maybe split a shank of venison. The Coe brothers, Doc Skurlock, John Middleton, TomO'Folliard lard, Jake Scoggins, Jim

French, Charlie Bowdre and a few others that he didn't know by name. Billy Bonney, one of Sheriff Brady's executioners, was with them, too.

The shooting started before Robey's bunch got to the place where the others were. It broke out when Charlie Bowdre fired point-blank from the hip and sent a slug through Buckshot Roberts's body. From way across the clear space, Clay saw the small puff of dust burst out from Buckshot's clothing, and he saw him return the fire with the rifle before he staggered inward and slammed the door. After that it was a state of siege.

Everybody made for the brush and cover. Clay took the roan horse back among the trees and staked him out with his riata. He had a sick, weak feeling in his middle. He tried to think that this was not really happening, but he knew it was. He had a notion to mount right up again and ride on out, and to hell with everything, but he knew he couldn't. Robey Moore was there to see to that.

'You come along with me, Forrest,' he said after he got his horse picketed the way he liked it. 'We're goin' to spread out in these trees, here, and you can come along with me. I aim to get you some good, clean shootin'.'

Clay went along. He left the Winchester in the scabbard and hoped Robey wouldn't notice it. The Colt was enough for the shooting he felt he was going to do; he wouldn't have to fake poor shooting with it at the distance. Except for accident, Buckshot would be fairly safe from him.

They went through the trees and bellied down behind a hummock in the ground. When they could view the building once again Clay saw that Buckshot had gotten in some licks. He saw George Coe running through the trees with one hand streaming blood, a finger shot away. He saw John Middleton walking along there in the open like he had no particular place to go and wasn't sure from where he'd started. There was a big, red mess on his shirt and blood was coming from his mouth. He coughed and bubbles formed around his lips. He barely made cover before he toppled over in a heap.

Down behind the hummock, Robey Moore began to lever brass. Buckshot Roberts could not be seen, but Robey was firing into the building, anyway; indiscriminately, hoping for a hit. Watching him, Clay saw his face lying tanned and hard against the rifle stock. Robey's lips had a soft turn to them, remindful of his pleasant mood, as though there was nothing else he'd rather do. Clay wondered how a man could get that way; how a man could kill another human being just for the pleasure of it. Just like shooting pigeons in the trees.

The sun went higher and the siege dragged

on. During the frequent lulls in the firing, threats and imprecations were exchanged between both parties. Blazer's wife pled in vain for the sparing of Buckshot Roberts's life. In return Dick Brewer demanded that Roberts be ejected from the building, under threat of burning it. Doc Blazer then reminded Brewer that the mill was standing on federal land, and that anything like that would be receptive of drastic retribution. So nothing came of it.

They'd been there for hours and hadn't much to show for it. Buckshot Roberts was hurt bad, likely dying slow in there, but he was fighting, still. He had some armament and a mixture of fire was coming from the windows. Most of it was 44-40 rifle and pistol shooting, but now and then Clay would hear the big boom of an old Sharps buffalo gun. He kept hoping Roberts would connect with that.

He could tell that everyone was getting fidgety and impatient. Over a bit, he saw Dick Brewer discussing it with Scoggins and McNab and he knew that they were wearying. Pretty soon Brewer backed away and sneaked over under cover of the trees and brush. He flipped his hand at Clay and Robey as he passed in back of them.

'I'm goin' to get that bag of wind,' he said. 'He's done too much damage; he's actin' like he owns the place.'

Clay watched him edge away and when he

came in sight again he was down the line some, creeping up a pile of logs. He was shielded from the building, but Clay could see him fine. He could see the window from which Roberts fired mostly, and he had the feeling that something was going to come of this. It'd gone on too long and something was bound to break.

A kind of quiet had come over the fighting and Clay knew that everyone was waiting. He kept on watching Brewer and Buckshot's window, and he didn't care if Robey had his eyes on him or not. He knew his yearning for Roberts was showing in his face, but it didn't make any difference any more.

When Brewer opened fire Buckshot returned it, but nothing came of the first exchange. Brewer was too far down for Roberts to get a decent bead on him, and maybe he was pretty low to get a bead on Roberts, because he bellied up the pile some for the next one. That time he choppd a whisk of chips away from the window ledge, and the next time Buckshot edged into view Clay saw he held the Sharps. He took a long time in his sighting, and Brewer was spraying gunshot all around him; but when he pulled the trigger the gob of buffalo lead took the top of Brewer's head off.

The shooting all around picked up again and Clay got a light, exulting feeling into him. He knew what he was going to do. He pulled his revolver around and pushed it into Robey's ribs. Robey looked at him as though he saw him for the first time in his life.

'Come on with me,' Clay said to him. 'Leave the rifle and come with me.'

Robey made a blind move to swing the rifle, and Clay chopped at his arm with the pistol.

'I said to leave it. Leave it right there, and move.'

Clay backed off into the brush and Robey followed him. Robey was beginning to smile about it now, like there was a joke involved that had just occurred to him. He didn't even lose it when Clay took his pistol from him. It made Clay nervous and jumpy all over again and he had the notion that Moore was just as dangerous unarmed as the other way around.

He prodded Robey through the trees and toward the staked-out roan. They were moving quietly, but there was gunfire crackling around in there and it didn't make much difference. Clay's big fear was being spotted by someone idly looking through the brush, but the danger passed when they got beyond the firing line.

Clay got his riata coiled, and everything set without any trouble. 'So long, Robey,' he said when he was mounted. 'I rode with you like Pa said to do, but I don't hold with this. I'm finished now. I done my part.'

Robey's expression hadn't changed at all; he looked as though the whole thing was nothing but a prank to him. 'So long, Forrest. *Adiós.* I'll see you around some day. I'll look you up; I'll find you. You're mine, kid. You belong to me.'

'No, I don't,' Clay said. 'I belong to myself.'

But they were both wrong, anyway for a time they were; and Clay always remembered the irony of his saying that to Robey. He'd fired his last shot in the Lincoln County war, but still it reached to bind him in. For the next three years Clay was a possession of the government.

8

After Rusty Rhodes brought Diamond-Back in like that Clay couldn't keep his mind from re-examining all these old remembrances again. For a number of days thereafter the business up at Blazer's Mill was in his head so strongly he fancied he could hear the shooting sounding through the timber of that country, and smell the powder smoke in mixture with the pine scent. He kept remembering what Robey Moore had said to him when he'd coiled his rope and sat there in his saddle, his gun in Robey's face. He was not afraid of Robey, but Diamond-Back's appearance had filled him with a sense of urgency. He felt the shadows of his past seeping down upon him from the humped hills over west. He knew something was going to happen soon.

He had to fight it in his mind from day to day. He didn't wish to contemplate what might lie ahead for him, but reminders of the visitation were everywhere that he might choose to look. Ygenio was not so carefree any more in his expenditure of ammunition in his endless feud against the furtive coyotes. Rusty Rhodes never rode fence without his rifle free and easy in the boot. Apolinaria regarded every shade and shadow on the horizon with suspicion, and watched Abrana with increasing worry.

Soon, Clay knew, it would be time for her to leave. He didn't fight the notion any more. He accepted it because there was nothing else to do. What the hell, he'd worked it out, he had no cause to try and keep her here. He hadn't anything to offer her except the rag-tail end of a vendetta that had started while she was still a kid. But all this business had got him to thinking straight about her, anyway; so he'd know when the time came for him to take his hat in hand, as Hardin used to say. If the time came. If time just didn't end some day altogether, in a hammer stroke on a center-fire cartridge.

He took things easy with Abrana in the days after Diamond-Back was there, and it was like they were waiting for a sign to tell them when it was time for her to go. He did not try further intimacies with her and they avoided any repetition of the evening with the lights below them in the village. It was hard to reconcile himself to the necessity for doing this; when the fire was down in the dooryard and they were sitting on the gallery he would have great compulsions in that direction. But he knew what he was doing.

So they were pleasant and casual with each other and sometimes it was like they'd never gone down to see the lights at all that night. When there was time they'd ride along the low swells near the ranch together, simply enjoying the company of each other, and Clay would sometimes think that what had been personal between them was gone and never would come back. Until he might catch her watching him in secret, and he would realize that he had been regarding her in that way, too. So he knew that all this they were doing was nothing but a pretense, an expedient. It made him wish the world would bust right open, and get the whole thing over with.

Not more than a few days after the outlaw had shown himself Clay ran into Dodge Liston out there on his land. He hadn't thought much about Dodge and those others lately, but his meeting with him served to fix that person more firmly in his mind, and caused him to see Dodge's capabilities in a more respectful light. From a long ways off he saw Dodge crossing over from his own line, and it occurred to him that a hell of a lot of people had chosen to call upon him through his back door in that manner.

There was an arroyo handy and he ducked down into it to see what Dodge was going to do. Dodge was a slick sort of person and the more you found out about a man like that when he wasn't aware of it the better off you were. Dodge wasn't one to reveal much of himself when he knew that he was being observed and studied.

It was hot down there and Clay was damned uncomfortable. It was shortly after noon and the brassy sun beat down upon him like a mallet. The white alkali stirred up by the Morgan's hooves did not settle and carry off in the windless air, and he fought chokes and sneezes all along the way. There were prickly pear and sand burrs to add to his discomfort. But he stayed down in there anyway.

This slit in the baked earth was narrow, but maybe a quarter of a mile in length. He'd entered at the southern end of it, dismounted and crept up the sloping side to have a look around. He saw Dodge coming easily and taking his pleasant time about it. If he had any notion he was being watched he didn't show it.

He rode in the open like that for quite a while. Now and then he'd draw up and pause a spell, or maybe take a slanting cut to one side or the other of his general line of travel, as though he might be looking for a sign. It seemed like he had all day to spend out there. Finally, a line of low rises intervened, and Clay slid down the slope and walked further up the cut.

When he climbed up for another look around, Dodge had disappeared. Clay had a more commanding view from this new place than he'd had before, but that seemed to make do difference. The other man was as completely gone as though he'd never been there in the first place. It filled Clay with a sense of bafflement, and with a nagging irritation. The thought that a man could evade his eyes in such a way was not appealing. Such a thing could cost his life some time.

He stayed there for a time stretching his neck around like a wild turkey in the hills, and when he turned to slide back down again he was aware that Dodge was watching him. Dodge had somehow gotten around to the other side of the arroyo and was sitting his horse in a negligent way, and seeming to take an enjoyment in the proceedings down below. Having failed to watch his rear as he should have done made Clay feel like a damned fool by any count. But Dodge's subtle turning of his flank had taught him something new about that paunchy, well-dressed man, and he appreciated it.

'You lose something down there, Clay?' Dodge asked him from above. 'Don't seem a man'd wallow around in the heat of such a ditch unless he was looking for something.'

Clay slapped the dust out of his shirt and jeans and climbed aboard the roan horse, which had trailed him down the draw. They went in switchbacks to the top before he answered. He felt stiff and awkward, just like he was guilty of some indiscretion, like maybe he had belched in church.

'I might ask you the same thing,' he said when he was next to Liston. 'I might ask you what you was doin' over here when you got all that land of your own to ride around on. Don't seem you need this much room for exercise.'

He was sore and he didn't care just how he sounded. Dodge was sitting there all neat and cool and he had him at a disadvantage, and he ought to have some of that smugness ruffled.

'I guess I was lookin' for something at that,' Dodge Liston said. 'I was looking for a horse of mine. One of my wranglers said he saw one of my string over this way a few days back, and I thought I'd come over for a look. I didn't want to bother you by coming around in front, and asking did you see it.' Dodge squinted at the ground in heavy thought. 'This horse of mine was said to have a man upon it.'

Clay saw Diamond-Back riding off again, his hate like a slow fire in his face. 'I ain't got no horse of yours,' he said. 'Only horse been around here that ain't mine was one belongin' to Old Man Medford, and he's gone back long ago.'

Why was he lying to Dodge? Was he afraid of him? On his own land he was doing this and it made him boil inside to think about it. But Dodge had got him on the defensive, and there was no helping it.

'Feller that seen this horse said also that the rider looked mighty familiar to him,' Dodge went on. Dodge had now shifted his scrutiny to a Spanish dagger plant. 'Said he looked an awful lot like one of the old Moore crowd. Fact is, this wrangler of mine, who is renowned for the truth of his tongue and the sharpness of his eyes, is set to swear on the thickest Bible in the Pecos Valley, that this rider was a man known around as Diamond-Back.'

Clay got a grip on himself, and commenced to enter into the spirit of the thing. He'd been pushed around enough by Dodge, God damn it. 'Well, now, that could be,' he said, 'but I don't think I'd bet a lot on it 'cause I know about nearly everything that comes by here. Anyway, Diamond-Back's doin's ain't no affair of mine. I ain't had no truck with him for a longer time than I can think of just now. He might be dead, for all I know; and the rest of 'em, too, no matter what the tales you people bring me. Lots of fellers in their trade die sudden-like, you know.'

'I suppose it could have been his ghost, then,' Dodge said. 'But he surely had an eye for horse-flesh. That cayuse was one of my very best. I do surely miss him. Mighty fine riding horse, he was.'

That time Clay got himself a chuckle. The humor of the situation was appealing to him now. 'Now, it could have been his ghost, at that,' he said. 'I always knew Diamond-Back to be mighty choosy about his horses in his lifetime. No reason at all to expect him to change that just 'cause he's a ghost now, is there?'

'No,' Dodge said, 'I guess there ain't. It wouldn't fit his character at all.'

*   *   *

They rode on leg and leg down toward the ranch, and Dodge appeared to have forgotten about his missing horse for the moment, but Clay knew he hadn't done any such thing. He knew Dodge was playing himself a waiting game. Fellers like Dodge always had themselves two or three ways to approach a matter; and they were always sniffing around for another one. People like him had to have an eye upon them all the time.

'I expect you've been doing some thinking these days, Clay,' Dodge said after a time. 'You been grubbin' around here on your place for quite a few weeks now, and I was wondering if you gave any consideration to what you and me talked about before.'

'Well, puttin' it that way, Dodge, I been so

busy grubbin' I ain't had much time for anything like that,' Clay said to him. 'It takes a heap of time to work this place, and there ain't a hell of a lot left for thinkin' of that sort. You'd think a man'd grow to hate a place that took so much to handle, but you know I'm comin' to like it more every day.'

'You are? Even without help? Maybe so, but I tell you, Clay, you don't want to put it off too long. A man can find other places for his money out here.'

'I got help now,' Clay said. 'I got a feller named Rusty Rhodes with me now, and I'll no doubt get more when the time comes to do it.'

'Old Man Medford was talking about that the other day. We was playing cards in town— I remember it. He said Rusty never could pull his share of the load. Kind of a fly-by-night kid that never would amount to anything.'

'He's pullin' it for me, Dodge,' Clay said. 'I more or less expect it's in the spirit. Don't that sound reasonable?'

Dodge Liston turned his big bulk in the saddle. 'Listen, Clay, I ain't goin' to fool around with this thing forever. Others around here are a damned sight more het up about my horse goin' off than I am. They don't like the idea of Moore's takin' it in broad daylight and then comin' over on your land like that. They ain't sure that maybe you didn't know about it all the time.'

'If they've been thinkin' that, then let 'em

come around and say it. I'm gettin' kind of sick of all this whispering in the grass. It's been goin' on ever since I come home and I don't mind sayin' I don't like it one bit. There's been an endless line of folks comin' out to say how they don't want me here no more. I figure it's about time they either put up or shut up. What do you think, Dodge?'

They had come to a level place some distance above the buildings and Clay could see the small activity going on down there. A cooking fire was breathing its slight smoke through the kitchen chimney, and some of Abrana's things were moving gently on a wash line strung between the gallery posts—glory, she was always washing something! Somewhere, muffled by the buildings, a hammer's beat made a soft, thick sound. On the silver-gray ranch roof Rusty's new shingles stood out like freshly minted pennies in a handful of old, worn coins.

'I think you'd better pay more attention to what I've said, Clay; one of these days a bunch is liable to ride on out here and take you in tow. I'm offerin' to help you salvage something from this mess of yours, and you'd better listen to it. Be a sight better than bein' driven off the place. Or worse.'

'You figure they'd do a thing like that?' Clay asked.

'I wouldn't put it past 'em,' Dodge said. 'They're gettin' more impatient about it every day.'

'Really? I guess, then, I'll have to put you off again, Dodge. I just now nearly gave in to you, but your sayin' that changes everything again. I feel honor-bound to stick around long enough to see this community back its talk with action. It would be worth a lot to see that.'

Dodge rode off with his broad back straight, his rear end bulging around the saddle cantle, and his thick neck crimson beneath the brim of his hat. Clay took the roan horse down the slope to the house and turned him into the corral. Coming around to the dooryard he saw Apolinaria and Abrana watching through the kitchen window, and then he saw Ygenio and Rusty talking to a man sitting on a tall bay horse. This man sat easy and careless-like, and Clay saw Sam Chandler's face beneath the hat. Clay felt the don't-give-a-damn exuding from Chandler as he came across the sun-dappled court toward him; and right away he was conscious of the irritation rising in him.

'A great day for callers,' he said to Chandler. 'They come as fast as I can say hello to 'em. You'd almost think they had nothing else to do.'

'Chandler here says he wants to see you about something or other,' Rusty Rhodes said. 'I asked him what, but he wouldn't speak up. Wouldn't talk to us about it.'

Ygenio bored a hole in the earth with the toe of his boot. 'He say nothing. He sits there like a *bulto* and we look at one another. I think we maybe drive him off, but then we see you coming.'

Chandler's lips were curved and this served to goad Clay's exasperation. Chandler was sitting there and watching them as though he maybe owned the place, or anyway, was sometime figuring to.

'Well,' Clay said, 'I'm here. What in hell do you want me for?'

'I come to talk to you about a running iron,' Sam Chandler said. 'There was one picked up over at the Gallaghers' the other day. And we was curious to know if you had any idea as to who might be swinging a long rope around here.'

'Seems to me you ought to know more about that than me,' Clay said. 'You're the only one in the valley I know of that appears to have the time to stick his nose into other people's business. Why don't you take a flying guess?'

Chandler turned his head and watched the cottonwoods move their arms against the sky. The breeze blew softly up there among the crowns, but it was still and quiet in the dooryard.

'When they found this thing they ran a quick tally and figured there was maybe twenty-thirty head not to be accounted for.'

'Maybe them Gallaghers ain't learned how to count,' Clay said. 'They always did strike me as a little thick.'

Sam Chandler ignored this estimation. 'All prime stock taken off. No yearlings or anything like that; likely countin' on a quick turnover.'

'I wouldn't know how rustlers work,' Clay said. 'If it was me, now, I'd likely run the calves. I like the taste of that young and tender liver.'

'Now, that's a funny thing,' Sam Chandler said, 'because the brand they found was yours.' Chandler reached beneath the saddle blanket on the far side and tossed the short iron rod down to Clay, who caught it. 'Here, I brung it back to you. Kind of a waste to leave it lyin' out like that.'

Clay turned the brand over in his hands. It was the Pine Tree Brand, all right, just like Pa had fashioned it from memory of the big trees back there in the soft Missouri hills. But the hammer-work wasn't his. Clay kept his eyes on Chandler when he passed the iron to Ygenio.

'This one of yours, Ygenio?'

Ygenio considered it from all angles. 'No. No, it is not mine. I do not make them like this. I like to have a nice handle on the ones I make, and as you can see, this one is inferior. Yes, a nice handle is a very important thing.'

'I guess that's your answer, Chandler,' Clay said then. 'This thing don't belong here.

Looks like some blacksmith was havin' him some practice.'

'Could be it wasn't just a blacksmith,' Chandler said. Chandler was talking careful now, and not sitting with so much swagger.

'You better git,' Clay said quietly. 'I'm tired of seein' your face comin' into this place. I don't think you better come back again.'

Sam Chandler eased his big bay horse around. 'Maybe I won't have no choice about it, Forrest. Folks have got themselves some anger now.'

'Let the folks move out, then,' Clay said. 'There's a big land out here and a lot of room to move around in. Me, I'm stayin' on. I like it here. Quite a bit.'

'Maybe you are stayin' at that,' Chandler said, and he nudged the belly of the bay. 'And then again, maybe you ain't.'

Clay held the iron in his hand and watched Sam Chandler ride on down the cottonwood lane. He had a nice sit to him, he was thinking; and he remembered the way that Robey always rode. He looked at the rod once more, turning it against the palm of his hand. It wasn't bad work, but it wasn't Pa's or Ygenio's.

'Damn Robey,' he said. 'I guess we know what went through that barranca now. Ain't many doubts about that.'

'Oh ho,' Ygenio said quietly. 'I think that, too, and I wonder if I am right.'

'Yeah, you're right.' Clay moved his head and looked away on off at the western hills, lounging in purple shadows on the far horizon. 'Yeah, it's Robey, all right; even rigged this brand to point our way. I reckon Diamond-Back wasn't foolin' none. I guess we got somethin' on our hands now.'

9

That was the beginning of it; or the end of it, if he chose to look at it in another way. The horse that Diamond-Back had taken, and the iron—with the Gallaghers' cattle going through the barranca, as they surely must have. Either way they were considered, the beginning or the end, the incidents seemed designed to point a finger of guilt at the Pine Tree spread.

Clay had known, if talk was to be believed, that Robey's crowd was giving the neighborhood his attention, but now he knew he was working it with a purpose. He remembered that Robey was never one to be long denied the things which he believed to be his own; by right or conquest, or by force of arms.

Examples of this came with freshness to his mind. Beyond Robey's common pilferings and killings, more exquisite forms of acquisition and revenge returned to Clay's remembrance. He recalled a Spanish girl that Robey had one time taken an earthy fancy to. Her father had kept a herd of sheep, and they lived together in the foothills of the Capitans, not far from Encinosa. This girl, whose name Clay could not recall, was inclined to view Robey's interest with enthusiasm, an enthusiasm not shared by her *pariente*. And in that Spanish household, the father's word was law.

His objections did not meet with sympathetic understanding on the part of Robey Moore. Robey's attitude was singular and predatory in the matter. He saw what he desired and what he wanted he must surely have. It might have been a simple thing for him to induce the sloe-eyed girl to ride on out with him, and to hell with what her father said. But Robey enjoyed a game when he had the leisure to pursue it; and he was out to make that sheepman eat his words.

Among the accouterments of his trade, Robey possessed a bowie knife of rarest edge and beauty. Clay recalled that he would sometimes sit before an evening campfire and hone it on his boot-sole by the hour. One night Robey took that razor's edge and crept in among the Spanish father's sheep. By the light of a full Orange moon he cut the lives from eleven of those woolly throats. On the following evening he made mutton of half a dozen more.

113

He employed himself thuswise for a number of nights, and in the end he got the Spanish father's palsied blessing. He got the warm-fleshed girl, as well, for all the pleasure either one derived from it. Four days later she was shot from the saddle in a running fight which roared through Baca Canyon. And Clay recalled that Robey had not even returned to bury her.

Clay knew that Robey was out to get him now. He recognized his hand of ruination in everything that was going on around him. His previous naïveté in the matter seemed incredible now in recollection, and he wondered why he'd ever thought that Robey would leave him to his own life. Just now that seemed a vain and pious hope, and it was incredible that he'd considered that things might go as he had planned for them when he'd come down from Vegas. For now no ranch in all that valley was left unmolested or unvisited, save his own, and Clay no longer wondered that the people thereabouts regarded him with hate and fear. With Robey, vengeance was an art and passion.

Clay knew that something was going to break. Robey's teeth were drawing blood and the wrath occasioned by these depredations was heightened for the victims by the knowledge that the Forrest property was left scrupulously inviolate. Posses formed and bands of armed men went searching through

114

the countryside. There could have been an element of humor in that for Clay, because he knew that Robey couldn't be caught like that. But, instead, it had a chilling quality for him; he didn't know but what those same law-enforcing bodies might turn at bay and work their wrath on him. He knew that guns in concert were inclined toward recklessness.

*   *   *

Clay stood in the dooryard with the reins of the red roan horse and those of a buckskin mare in his hands and listened to the sounds that emanated from the house. Maybe he hadn't been standing there quite as long as it seemed, but he was aware of being impatient with Apolinaria for the length of time required to sermonize Abrana on her behavior up in White Oaks, and to help her pack her fiber case. It seemed, by God, that she never would let Abrana go, and sure as hell was hot this would be the one day when the westbound stage from Roswell would be on time, if not ahead of it. It was enough to make a man sit down and bite his nails. Waiting there like that, he was vaguely conscious of the luster of the day; of the little subtle messages which the cool and early morning air was circulating. There seemed to be a touch of autumn in it, though a man would have to pay strict attention to the

115

sundry signs to be certain in his mind.

An idle glance might tell him that the cottonwood leaves were losing just a bit of greenness, that some day not far off they would awaken into golden flame. And that tassel-eared squirrel over there, hadn't he been carting off those piñon, overlooked on the gallery? He knew what was up, all right. Still, there weren't many signs down here yet; not in this valley on the plains. In the mountains, now, it would be different. The chill nights, and slow sun in the days, would be making changes right and left. That would be a thing to see.

Abrana came out so quietly that she was standing next to him before he was aware of it. He was trying to think how he would offhand suggest this ride while Ygenio was roping the team and hitching up the wagon; when there she was, standing there and looking at him in a way that confounded all of his carefully planned imaginings.

'It is early,' Abrana said to him. 'Do we go so soon? And where is the wagon?'

'The wagon?' Clay said. 'Oh—Ygenio's got to hitch it up. I figured we might take a little ride around before we took you out to the road. What would you think of that?'

'Ride?' She looked surprised in saying this, and then her expression changed to one which seemed half-pitying, as though there was something he had failed to understand, and she was being sorry for him. 'But I have a skirt on. See? You should have told me.'

And so she had, Clay saw; and a white blouse with fine drawnwork up around the neck of it, and a curious sort of colorful, woven jacket over it. The effect of everything was very fine indeed, but his own stupidity dominated his feeling about her appearance.

'Well, what's the difference?' he said. 'I won't look.' He tried to sound light and pleasant, but he didn't feel it.

'Do not be angry,' Abrana said. 'It is not that. I was not thinking of that. Apolinaria will not think it proper for me to ride like this.'

'Let's forget about Apolinaria this one time,' Clay said, and he was conscious of his voice being tight and his throat strained.

Abrana watched him carefully. 'All right,' she said quietly. 'I do not like to displease her, that is all. Which horse shall I ride?'

Clay did not know whether he felt better or not. He knew he'd won a point, but he recognized it as a victory under pressure. It did not seem gallant to do a thing like that and he'd have to try to please her now that he'd hurt her feelings; but they were riding on the grasslands behind the house, Abrana on the roan, before he could think of anything to say.

'That's a pretty jacket you've got there,' he said at last; and he knew he'd hit it right because she smiled in appreciation.

'Thank you. It is from a Chimayo blanket. I made it one time when the blanket was very old and worn. It has the real *bayeta* in it,' she added.

'My,' Clay said. 'It surely does look fine.'

Clay did not know what *bayeta* was, nor was he even sure that he knew much about Chimayo except that it was an old Spanish village up somewhere above Santa Fe, but he did not admit that. In fact, he wasn't thinking any more about the jacket, but was savoring the effect of his discovery that a man could right himself with a woman if he commended her upon the way she looked. It was a valuable thing to know and his mood improved because of it.

But they were quiet during most of the ride. It was difficult to be jovial and hearty when he didn't feel it, and once it was established that Abrana was not put out with him he didn't feel compelled to talk. He'd never been good at masking his feelings, and he knew that Abrana was as knowing of that by now as he, himself, was. And it would only make her feel badly and unhappy if he talked the way he really felt. So he did not say much.

But the quiet between them made him feel more acutely the presence of her by his side, and a pace or two behind. She had been careful to maintain that position from the time they'd left the dooryard, and she didn't change it. It was not false modesty with her, or any kind of coyness, as he might have thought before he came to know her well. She was not at all ashamed of her browned legs, bare and smoothly round clear on up to where the black skirt stretched tightly across her thighs. To display them in a dance was quite all right, and to be expected, but to do so on the saddle of a horse was quite another thing.

It was hard for a man to work that out clearly in his head, but that's the way she was, and Clay accepted it.

They rode out nearly to the arroyo where Clay had come upon Dodge that day, and then cut back along the rise that lay behind the buildings. When they were almost due north of them Clay got down and helped Abrana from the roan. She looked at him with a question as he set her on the grass.

'I just wanted you to see this place all at once before you left; so you wouldn't forget it too soon.'

'I do not think I will do that easily,' Abrana said, but she turned her head and looked at the spread below them for a long time. 'I will not forget this place.'

'That's good. Take a long look, though. It's different in the mountains. I know.'

'That will not mean anything,' Abrana said. 'It is not the appearance of a place, but one's associations with it, that have meaning. Do you not know that?'

She was looking at him now. She had

removed the jacket and placed it around her, without her arms being in the sleeves. She was standing straight with her hands clasped at her waist and the jacket that way made her seem stocky and broad-shouldered. While this occurred to him, he wasn't thinking so much of the illusion as he was of the strength that this implied. It was in her posture, but more than that it was in her face as well. It held a line of youth and beauty in its construction, but the intelligence and candor of great maturity were in her eyes. Some women were like that, he thought suddenly. They never told half of what they knew; and what they knew had never been told to them in the first place. It was simply a part of them, like instinct maybe. And Abrana was one of these.

'Yes, I guess I know that,' he said, and he felt oddly small and no-account as he replied to her.

'Do not forget it,' Abrana said intensely. 'Ever.'

*　　　*　　　*

The rest of it was distasteful to him. He never did like to make good-byes, and a big fuss over a departure was always depressing somehow. It was best just to get it over with and done, and set about adjusting your life to the new idea of being minus the person who was leaving. Maybe some of that feeling was due to a kind of unintended callousness that all the fighting in the past years had conditioned in him, but he couldn't tell about that. Mostly, he thought, it was simply because of his natural reticence; he didn't like to make an occasion of it the way that some folks did.

Take Apolinaria as a case in point. Though she wasn't going more than half a mile beyond the house she was fitted out like she was maybe going to make the journey clear to White Oaks, and maybe take in a wedding and a wake to boot. She didn't have many opportunities to set herself out in her best and oldest, which was all the same, and when she did have one she made the most of it. Now, as she sat on the high wagon seat, her ancient lavender dress fell in copious folds about her legs and ankles. Her pointed black shoes caught the sun, reflecting it. Her black rebozo, green with age, draped from her head to waist, and was gathered in her hands.

A man didn't know whether to laugh at her or weep.

Rusty Rhodes, in clean Levis and a washed, sun-bleached shirt, came forward with his hat in one hand and a bouquet of wild flowers in the other; and with an air of ceremony, he presented these to Abrana, who smiled as she accepted.

'I'm surely sorry to see you go, Abrana,' Rusty said to her. 'And I hope you'll come on back again soon.'

'Thank you,' Abrana said. Her head was bent as she sniffed the flowers and Clay could see the deep cedar lights glinting in her hair. 'Columbine,' she said of the wild flowers. 'And lupine; and two Spanish roses. You must have looked hard for these; it is late.'

'Oh, there's a few around,' Rusty said. 'Mavericks, I guess. I kind of marked the places in my mind. It wasn't no trouble.'

'They are very beautiful,' Abrana said. 'Thank you.'

'It's all right,' Rusty said, and whatever else he might have had to say was lost in the sound of Ygenio emerging from the house and climbing onto the wagon seat. By the time Abrana was up between him and Apolinaria, Clay was mounted, and they headed out; except for Rusty, who remained where he was and waved his hat slowly in a wide arc.

Clay was hoping that Apolinaria would forget about Abrana on the horse, but he should have known she wouldn't. It would be out of character for her to compromise on a thing like that, even though Abrana was going away. He felt half-inclined to get into it himself, but something warned him that no one but a fool would intrude himself into a discussion between two women.

'You should not ride a horse in that manner,' Apolinaria began in a level tone which carried above the sound of the trace chains and the creaking wheels.

122

'In what manner is that?' Abrana asked. She watched the roadway straight ahead.

'In the manner I see you riding behind the house. Nakedly. It is indecent.'

'I did not ride it nakedly,' Abrana said. 'And it was not indecent.'

'A young girl should have shame to do a thing like that. Are my teachings wasted? Your *parientes* would turn in their graves if they were to know.' Apolinaria crossed herself devoutly. 'With a man, to make it worse.'

Clay looked at the two struggling with each other's minds upon the wagon seat. Apolinaria's rebozo was clenched in her big hands, and Abrana's lips were tight with little white dents pressing at the corners. He had a strange feeling about this business.

'I am not a young girl now,' Abrana said. 'I am a woman and I shall ride a horse as I please. And my *parientes* would not have shame for me were they to know; it was not just any man with whom I rode. It is important that you know that.'

For the first time since this had all begun Clay saw Abrana turn to face Apolinaria. He saw in her eyes the same thing he'd seen less than half an hour ago when they were standing up behind the buildings and she had taught him something he hadn't known before.

It seemed now that Apolinaria was learning something new herself, or perhaps receiving confirmation of something she had feared and had fought by consequence. But Abrana's force of presentation was making her accept it now, and that was significant for Clay. He did not understand everything about the long look that passed between them, but when their gazes shifted once again to other things he knew that Abrana had established herself as a person in her own right. She had passed a kind of milestone and everybody knew it.

Clay loped ahead when he saw the long dust snaking upward from the valley floor. From far off he could see the lumbering stage and the four horses, coming up in miniature. When they went from sight behind the swells of land they kept from view a long while, and when they reappeared it was sudden and explosive, where the road crested all at once and leveled out; the clatter and the pounding first, and then the sight of them. Colli Johnson standing in his old boots and sawing at the reins. The long blacksnake coiled around his shoulder and his rough face animated in profanity at his animals, as the bits hauled them from the gallop. To a nervous walk; to a full, head-tossing halt.

Clay swung down and walked over to the boot. Colli Johnson's face was powdered with dust and his eyes were red and watery in the deep seams and valleys which made a relief map of his features.

'I got a passenger for White Oaks,' Clay

said to him. 'You got room?'

'Lots of it. Yours is the first. Ain't got no one yet. Maybe some at Hondo, or Lincoln. Won't know 'til I get there, though.' The exertion with the horses caused Colli Johnson to speak in short, breathy phrases.

'All right,' Clay said. 'It's a girl. Abrana Martinez. See you take care of her.'

'A girl? I'll surely take care of a girl. I don't get many of them on this run. I brought some up from the Texas line not so far back, but you wouldn't hardly call them girls. They're dancin' in Roswell now; and other things, too, if the truth was known.'

The thought of the girls in Roswell seemed to cause Colli to forget his breathlessness, and Clay was forced to interrupt his reflections on them.

'Well, this one ain't nothin' like that,' he said. 'So you give her good treatment; not too many damned bumps.'

Colli Johnson took this in as he examined the popper on his twenty-foot whip, then changed the subject when Clay was finished.

'I heard a friend of yours got it the other day, Clay. They found Bob Fergus dead up on the Bonito.'

'He ain't no friend of mine,' Clay said. 'As far as I'm concerned, that's good news. Who's this "they"?'

'A bunch from Lincoln. They was out huntin' deer; he was hangin' from a tree. Been dead quite a few days. That's all I know.'

Clay would have liked to learn more about Bob Fergus, but the wagon just then came bumping up the road. Ygenio brought the horses to a standstill, and then got down to help the women out. Clay went around to get Abrana's fiber case and after he had put it in the boot he handed Abrana into the carriage. It went quick and that's the way he wanted it.

Sitting in the corner like that, she looked forlorn and lonely, strangely out of place. It made him wish that he could comfort her, but he knew he couldn't because he felt so awkward now. Part of this was the presence of Ygenio and Apolinaria, who were next to him and talking, but another part of it was his own restraint at the whole idea of Abrana going away like this; and he wished to hell that it was over. He couldn't think of an intelligent thing to say to her.

When they backed away from the door, Colli Johnson let the blacksnake coil off to the ground, and looked around to make sure that everything was clear.

'All right,' Clay said. 'Take it easy, Colli.'

'Sure, Clay,' Colli said. 'Take it easy yourself. They're hot in town for you.'

'I know,' Clay said. 'Go ahead.'

The blacksnake drifted back, picked up speed, swung high and streaked forward with the popper exploding above the heads of the leaders. The animals braced and lunged against the traces and the carriage crashed ahead in motion. Colli Johnson's 'Yahoop! Yahoop!' made a sharp sound in the massive noise, and the dust swam high in the air again.

Clay stood in the center of the road until the stage lurched around a bend, and then he walked back to Apolinaria, whose face was crumpled into silent grief. Without thinking of it, he put his arm around her shoulder and snugged her head against his chest while she dabbed at her eyes with the fringe of the old rebozo. Just then it seemed a natural thing to do, and the quiet irritation he had felt with her was gone.

Her own gentle acquiescence to the gesture explained to him that everything was the same between them once again, with one exception. For the first time in his remembrance, her manner indicated a dependence upon him—a reversal of an older order. It was a new relationship that now existed; he had passed a kind of milestone of his own.

10

Clay came inside with the coffee cup and set it on the table in the kitchen where it would be handy to Apolinaria when she washed the dishes. Then, because he felt she'd been badly used of late, he hung around and chatted with her.

'That's fine coffee,' he said to her. 'Nothing like good coffee on a chilly morning like this one is.'

Apolinaria nested the empty cup into the others on the stack of breakfast dishes. 'I think that is why you flatter me,' she said. 'The coffee is no different than before. It simply tastes better because of the cold.'

Clay leaned against the table and entered into the spirit of it. 'I think your modesty will be the death of you some day,' he said. 'Nobody makes coffee like you do; it's mighty good stuff regardless of the weather. Many's the time I wished I had a cup of it in my craw.'

'Ho!' Apolinaria said. 'Now you are a chicken. Before I think you are an eagle, but now you are a chicken. Which is it?'

Clay knew he was being mocked, but Apolinaria's humor was obscure. She was a person to be wary of sometimes.

'What do you mean by that?'

'You are an eagle with Abrana, and now you are a chicken with your craw.' Apolinaria said this with an inflection of light amusement. 'Of course, an eagle may have a craw as well, for all I know of such a bird,' she added.

Clay moved around to the side where he could see her dusky face more clearly. A man would think there would be some kind of indication in her features, but there wasn't.

He wondered if she was being cynical.

'You ain't still put out with me about that, are you?'

Apolinaria shook her dark head in the manner of all those who have met the inevitable and have recognized it for what it is. 'I might as well be put out with the good *Dios* himself. It is not your fault. Nor is it that of Abrana. It is simply the way it is, that is all. I bow my head to it.'

'Well,' Clay said, and he turned it over in his mind while he got used to it. 'Well.'

It was something he would like to talk about with her, but her attention had already proceeded to matters beyond the business of Abrana. It seemed that she had nothing more to say about it. 'Will you tell Ygenio that I have a list of things he is to get in town?'

Clay adjusted himself to the new trend in the conversation. 'You can tell me,' he said. 'I'll go. I want to look around down there anyway. Make it short, though.'

'Short? Will you not take the wagon?'

'No, I'll ride,' Clay said. 'I don't think we ought to stock up too much just now. Enough for a week or two'll be all right.'

'So,' Apolinaria said softly, and she turned around and looked at him. 'Now you are thinking I may be right. It took you a long time.'

'I know,' Clay said. 'I'm kind of thick, I guess. What can we get by with?'

'We should have some coffee. And flour. And a side or two of bacon. Did Rusty kill the beef?'

'Yes; it's hung now. He did it yesterday.'

'Then two of the bacon will be enough. Even one might do if you have trouble carrying everything.'

'That's all right,' Clay said. 'I'll just throw it all in a sack and tie it on somewhere. It won't be no trouble.'

'All right, you do as you please,' Apolinaria said.

Clay went outside again and headed off toward the corral and barn. It was warm enough now to be out there without a jacket if you were in the sun, but the shadows still had a nip to them even if it was mid-morning. Over there against the barn wall the hollyhocks were getting a dried-out bedraggled look to them, and the delicate and fragile-looking morning-glories hardly dared to unfold themselves at all these days. And the trees seemed to be paling out somewhat more than they had when Abrana left a week ago. Fall was coming on, all right, and one morning they'd awaken and see the cold fire of those cottonwoods burning golden all along the alley to the road.

Coming out of the shed with his saddle and other gear, he went into the corral and whistled for the roan, which came over to him slowly and indecisively, making a little game of his own maneuvering. By the time Clay had the bit in his mouth Ygenio came by with his riata to rope the wagon team, but Clay stopped him before he shook his loop.

'Don't bother about them,' he said. 'I'll go in; we don't need much.'

'No? I thought we needed quite a lot. Did you get the list from Apolinaria?'

Clay went around and heaved the saddle onto the Morgan's back, adjusted it on the blanket and kneed the belly softly as he drew the cinch. 'Yeah. We just ain't loadin' up, that's all. We're goin' to live from week to week for a while. Until we see how things get on.'

'Oh ho.' Ygenio hung the coiled riata on a post and began to roll a cigarette. 'Well, there is no need for you to go. I had planned on it, as always, so I can do it even so.'

'No, that's all right. I'll go. I know you get a kick out of goin' on them buyin' sprees but I want to have a look around. I ain't been down in a while, and I ought to see if folks are as hot for me as Colli said they were.'

'Well, all right,' Ygenio said, and there was a silence while he lit his cigarette. 'Will you be long?'

'Don't figure to be,' Clay said. 'Anyway, I hope not. You got something you can do around here 'til I get back? I might have some news and I don't want to have to chase all over for you.'

Clay finished with the saddling, swung the gate open and led the horse outside. Ygenio stroked the red roan's nose as Clay swung up, then stood there, smiling up at him.

'Well, there are still a few steers to be made,' he said with humorous delicacy. 'They were missed before.'

'All right. You do that then. You got creosote? And how about Rusty? You ought to have him for that.'

'He went to look around. He is always looking around these days, but he will be back. We have plenty creosote,' Ygenio added.

'All right,' Clay said. 'I'll try to make it back in early afternoon. Maybe sooner. *Adiós.*'

'*Buenos días,*' Ygenio said, and he touched his sombrero with the hand that held the cigarette.

*   *   *

Heading off, the thoughts of going down to town got into Clay. The more he contemplated the angry mood of that place the less he liked it; but someone had to do it. Until now it had always been Ygenio's pleasure to make that frequent trek, but the time had come when Clay couldn't let him take the risks that were attendant on it. The element of danger was too great these days, and sending Ygenio off like that, no matter how he liked to go, would only run the chance of exposing him to an unprovoked attack. Too many people had blood in their eyes around that place.

So he had to go himself. He had to go himself, and while the prospect of it was not the enjoyable and expectant thing he used to experience many years ago, there was still a quality of wonder in it when he considered all the changes time had wrought. Just like Dodge and all the others said, that town was growing up. It was away past the fondest hopes that either Murphy or McSween had had for Lincoln in the old days, and if the railroad came there'd be no end of it.

From a kind of cattle-crossing near the Pecos, it had sprawled and otherwise gotten out of hand to a point where the oldtimers would no longer recognize it. Among other things, ambitious and knowing people were putting the rivers to work. A man was one time content to sit up there on the high ground when the day's work was done and watch the Pecos and the Hondo carry on their never-ending dreams, or maybe curse at them and stomp around some when they went dry as they had a mind to off and on. But now these folks were digging ditches and plowing the lowlands and electing one another major-domos of the new acequias. And on top of that there was a whole new crowd down there, a shopkeeping, store-building crowd, that would sell you anything that you could think

133

of, and like as not a thing or two that had never occurred to you at all. They had called it Roswell, now, for more than half a decade.

And going down there now, he was very conscious of these alterations. They somehow intensified this feeling that he had of being on the outside of everything down there, and looking in. It was nothing like the old times when he would tag along with Hardin and Ygenio in the spring wagon on a shopping tour.

A person could look for miles in that bygone day and see little more than bunch grass, rolling plain and level river-flat. But now his eyes were filled with man's creations in any direction he might choose to look; sod-busting everywhere, homes and cabins on the water courses, shiny barbed wire streaking off in long, glinting lines. A far cry from those adobe heaps that Van Smith had fathered long ago. And now Pat Garret tinkering with artesian wells, they said; and the possibility of the railroad coming in. It was enough to make a memory-minded oldster shake his head.

Clay rode on down with his revolver on his hip. He didn't have his nose jointed up for trouble, but a person never knew. It sometimes seemed that those who wanted peace the most were those who got the least of it. And he wasn't taking any chances.

Despite the feel of autumn in the air, it was hot down in those streets, and crowded. Up on the high ground beyond the town a slow breeze cooled the day, but here the atmosphere was warm, and thick with dust. And there was more humanity, and more contrivances for carting it about, than he'd ever seen before at any one time, except for those he'd seen in Santa Fe; rigs, traps, steel-rimmed wagons and wooden-wheeled *carretas*, all kicking up their share of dirt. And the people that rode around in some of those things—well, Gawdalmighty.

There was nearly every sort of person he had ever thought of, and they all seemed to be in a rush. All going somewhere, or coming from someplace else. A lot of them were country people, Spanish folk, cattlemen, ranchers and the like; but a good many more weren't, or anyhow, didn't appear to be.

These others were *neuvos*, as their clothes surely told him; none of that riggin' had come from around there. They were imported things, likely, from far-off Kansas City or Chicago even. Fellers walking here and there, or riding in a light trap, as their fancy pleased them, wearing slick gray trousers and a checkered vest, and maybe a gold watch chain across the middle of it; with knee-high shiny boots, and all topped off with a big hat near as high as the smokestack of that Santa Fe locomotive that he'd rode behind. Nothing missing but the sparks and smoke.

And the womenfolk, glory be. Prancing

along the boardwalks and underneath the building galleries just like prideful fillies. Womenfolk wearing little scraps of high-laced black shoes and flimsy print dresses, thin and swishy, maybe giving off a hint of what was underneath. With bonnets on their heads, tied beneath the chin with a pretty ribbon, and a scooplike brim coming out over their faces, that made a man curious to peek around inside. And parasols for shading out the sun, and like to poke your eye out if you got too close or didn't watch where you were going.

He wondered how his ma would take to all this business if she was alive again to look at it; his ma and her linsey-woolsey, and her flat-heeled shoes. That was back a time, all right.

*   *   *

He did what he had come to do, and then he hung around a bit. He had a mind to sample the temper of the town, and anyway, a man didn't get to see sights like these so very often unless he lived here in the middle of it all, something that Clay didn't hanker after. It was all right to have a town like this handy and near by to come to when a person had the inclination, but he surely wouldn't want to make it permanent; not with all these people pushing him around, nor this never-ending racket that didn't have a silent place to think in; with all those slops and garbage spilling out of windows. It was a good place to amuse yourself in now and then, but he wouldn't want to live there.

With the provision sack fastened to the cantle, Clay tied the red roan to a hitch-rack midway along the street, and mixed with the moving crowd, keeping small and inconspicuous. He kept his mouth shut and his eyes open, and he saw a lot of people that he knew.

Rocking on the front veranda of a newly built hotel, Old Man Medford passed the time of day with a pair of Levi-wearing punchers. In an upstairs window, not far along the street, Clay got a glimpse of Dodge Liston palavering with a person in an office he kept there in town. Even at that distance Dodge looked smooth and composed, as though the heat and dust showed him a special consideration. Through a swinging batwing, he saw Steve Gallagher dealing in a card game. Jack Harris sat across from him, waiting for his hole card. On the boardwalk near the entrance, serape-shouldered field hands gossiped musically in Spanish.

Clay kept on walking. He went slowly down the street, crossed over and came back up along the other side. He passed below the gallery roof that shielded Dodge from the eyes of those directly underneath, wondering what kind of cunning thing Dodge was hatching up above. He sauntered past the hotel veranda, and from the tail of his eye saw Old Man Medford bring his rocker down and take his feet from the rail as he went by. He kept on going and didn't look back. Let the old coot wonder.

There were knots and groups of people all around, like sandbars in a river bed, and he was into the one that had the trouble waiting for him before he recognized it or could do anything about it.

A handful of men, maybe half a dozen, give or take a couple, was lazing and talking on the wide front stoop of a mercantile establishment. Some sitting, some standing, some halfway in between, simply gazing empty-eyed at whatever caught their fancy. Screwing up a leer when a leg went by. Spotting up the dust and planking with, tobacco spittle. Clay heard a laugh as he went through, and then a man with a wide, coarse face, and voice appropriate to his appearance, said, 'Damned if it ain't Clay Forrest. You bring Robey with you?'

Clay stopped dead and turned around; he maybe should have run right then, but he stopped instead. He turned around and looked this big man over. The man was one of those who take it on themselves to make a show of bravado with any man of reputation or notoriety; one of those who run up a gunman's score. Clay saw this all at once, and he saw that he was halfway drunk as well; and stupid in the eyes and loud in the mouth because of it. Grinning now, like he maybe attached a special importance to himself because he'd spoken out.

Clay looked him over close. He was mad inside. He saw this big-mouthed man and he knew he was a trouble-hunter. He wore a greasy buckskin jacket with fringe on the sleeves, and his hair cut long and matted to his shoulders. He was shy a few teeth, his nose was flat and he had an odor like an unswept stable.

'What do you want with me?' Clay said to him.

'Nothin', pal; I was just pointin' you out to the boys, here, that's all.'

'All right, they've had their look.'

The man moved so he stood in front of Clay.

'Any argument to my walkin' through here?' Clay said. He was feeling jumpy now. He could see the business shaping up.

The coarse-faced man hooked his splayed thumbs in a wide gun belt, and Clay wondered how simple this guy really was.

'Some might have objections, given they knew who you was.'

'You one of 'em?'

They were three, maybe four, feet apart, facing one another in the center of the stoop. The others were becoming more attentive now. Clay could feel them easing off and

139

making room the way that some men did when there was shooting imminent and they were being careful of it. He knew the big man was the gun hand in the crowd, boozer though he seemed to be. The others wouldn't have the stomach for a part of it, 'less it was sidewinding from a far-off place of safety. He wasn't afraid of anything from them.

The big man let his eyes drift around before he spoke again. 'I could be one,' he said then. 'We like a clean town here. I could be one, all right, Forrest.'

Clay let his shoulders loosen up. Crazy thoughts were running through his head. How in hell had this thing happened to him? What a lousy way to go if this lout got him. Would his hammer fall on a live round or on an empty chamber? What about this guy, was this a trap of some kind? Was there maybe another drawing a bead on his back from an upstairs window across the street? He damned near turned around to look.

'You better make your mind up,' he said. 'I ain't got all day.'

It happened fast. For all his great size and seeming muddleheadedness, the big man moved quick. The waiting quiet seemed like an endless stretch of time to Clay, and then it all broke open as the big one moved and the high-faced buildings threw the guns' roar back at him. Clay felt the blast of hot concussion smash him with a soft blow all over and he felt his revolver bucking in his hand, and then he saw the rough face of the big man go dreamy-slack and saw his body turn and walk without conscious life a few steps toward nowhere, and then fold into itself on the boardwalk.

Clay looked warily around as the sound echoed off into the sudden silence of the street. He felt the new shock get into everyone, and he held his gun level in his hand as those around pushed a wide alley, and he went through and commenced to run across the street. He got to the roan and swung on up. He'd like to hurry, but he knew he couldn't yet. He saw all those people gaping at him, but he couldn't hurry now. Too many horses in the way; too many people running senselessly about; too many rigs and wagons stopping in wondering astonishment.

He walked the roan toward the nearest side street and no one tried to stop him. It seemed that discretion was the better part of valor just then, and though wise plans were likely in the making nothing was done about his immediate apprehension. He had a clear road ahead. Spurring down the side street toward the open country up beyond, he glanced back once and saw the crowd closing in around the stoop of the mercantile store. A curl of smoke drifted up, and before his view was blocked he saw the dead man's clothing burning. That buckskin ought to make a fine stink, it occurred to him.

141

11

Clay put the horse on a dead run out of town. He'd started something now, all right. Things had been sitting in a kind of doubtful balance, and a touch in the right direction might have tipped things in his favor; but they weren't that way any more. Whatever balance had existed was now knocked all to hell and gone.

Those around who were waiting for a surefire provocation to jump him surely had their cue to move. It made no difference that the boozer'd been the one to start the business; that was all done now, and those in town who had a mind for it, had what they were looking for. Damn those bastards, Clay thought. Damn those troublemakers; a body just couldn't have no peace no matter what he done to get it. Wasn't any way to live his life as he saw fit to. There was always someone, somewhere, out to spoil it for him.

And they'd be coming now. In the name of law and order and several kinds of social justice they would soon be riding out. As soon as they got organized, they would; and everything was changed again. Damn that drunken lout.

He followed the Lincoln road, urging the Morgan on. The horse was going in ground-devouring strides, but still it seemed that everything was standing still. His mind went back to the day he'd waited for the carriage coming up the height of land from Roswell, and he remembered how long a time had been required for it to reach the entrance to the dirt trail leading to the alley. It almost seemed that he was traveling slower than that coach, riding out to home again, and he wondered what the cause of that illusion might be. He wondered if the thin edge of panic might be knifing into him.

He kept on looking back, but nothing followed. He had no idea how much time those people down there in town would need to organize a posse. Since it must be clear to them that they'd be hunting just one man they wouldn't lack for volunteers—the odds weren't bad against them—but still they'd require time. And they couldn't travel fast together.

Altogether, he considered, he might have half an hour's start on them, maybe more if he was lucky. There would be talk and reconstruction of the incident; there would have to be some depositions made. And since they now preferred to have their law all neat and legal there would have to be a warrant signed against him; and the posse members deputized. All the folderol would likely paralyze intended action for a while, and the chance existed that he might have an hour on them.

143

By the time he swung into the alley he had thought it out. He had a fair idea of what they'd have to do. He couldn't tell how such a thing would sit with Ygenio and Apolinaria, but when he saw them waiting in the dooryard they looked as though they'd maybe had a premonition of some kind, the way that people of that blood and breeding sometimes did. People of the land and soil, he thought detachedly, those near to God and nature, sometimes seemed to get a message from far off. So he knew they'd understand it.

When Clay swung down Ygenio watched him carefully, and spoke with hesitation. 'We see you coming fast, Clay,' he said. '*Si*, we see you coming fast and there is trouble, *no?*'

Clay looked around him while he got his breath. Already he seemed far away from this place, looking back at it, or maybe seeing it in his memory. It seemed to lose reality, just gazing at it, as he was.

'All kinds of it, I reckon,' Clay said. 'Had a scrap in town. Killed a feller, a big, drunken gun-tough that was hangin' around in there.' It all came out in scenes and pieces as he explained it to them. It seemed that it was far away, that none of it was real. But he knew it was.

Ygenio's face went quickly old and Apolinaria simply stood there, listening, and watching them, and waiting for what she likely knew must come. She didn't show anything in

144

her face at all. Just like a wall, Clay thought, looking at her. Even her eyes were silent.

'Well,' Ygenio said, 'I think we fight, then. Yes, we will have to fight.' There was a question in it.

Clay took his eyes from Apolinaria and looked at the trees crowning overhead. It was going to be a colorful fall, he thought. He surely would like to stick around and see it happen.

'No,' he said in a moment. 'No, we ain't goin' to fight no one. We wouldn't have a chance against 'em all for one thing, and for another I don't want to antagonize 'em any more than they already are. I got a notion they'll be acting pretty much in haste, and fighting them'll only make it worse. So we got to get out for a while; 'til this thing simmers down. We got to have time to find another way.'

Ygenio considered it in silence. He rubbed the elbow of his left arm. He fingered the brim of his sombrero. He rolled a small stone with the sole of his boot.

'Well, that may be best. I do not like to leave this place, for it is my home, but as you say, we cannot hope to fight them all. That would be a problem.' Ygenio kicked the stone away. 'When do you wish to go?'

'I think we better go right now,' Clay said. 'We may have an hour, but we can't count on that much. It's hard to say whether they'll track us or not, but we'll travel light just in case.'

For the first time Apolinaria entered into it. 'Get out? Leave this place now? I have dinner cooking. How can we leave at this hour?' She flapped her apron at a buzzing fly.

'Well, we got to go,' Clay said. 'We ain't got the time to sit around. You'll have to leave that dinner, I guess,' and he wondered why he was treating such an irrelevant thing so seriously. It must be Apolinaria's sensibilities, he thought; he wanted to lessen the brutality of it for her. 'We'll just take what I got in that sack, there, and leave the rest.'

'And live like the *bestias?*' Apolinaria demanded to know. 'What about my pots? My pans? And what will we sleep in?'

Clay hadn't thought it out that far, and he admitted it. 'For now we just got to get clear. We can think about all that later. But we got to get out first.'

'I have a relative whom we may go to,' Ygenio said after some thought. 'He is the husband of my older sister and he has a *casa* on the Lincoln road; it is just past Hondo.'

'Ah,' Apolinaria said. 'Some sense at last. Why did I not remember that?'

'All right,' Clay said. 'That'll do for the time being, anyway. We better get on with it, though. Where's Rusty?'

Ygenio turned his head and frowned toward the grassland rising upward beyond

146

the buildings. 'He is up there again. He came down to help with the steer-making, but then he goes up again. A while ago he thinks he maybe see someone up there, and we go together to look around, but there is nothing. When I come back he think he look a little more.'

'Oh, God,' Clay said. 'As if one thing ain't enough. Well, I'll chase him, then. You two get your things together and start moving out. I'll get back here as quick as I can, but don't wait. Take only what you need to get you up there. If I don't catch up with you I'll meet you there. But don't hang back, waitin' on me. You never know what these guys coming up may do.'

'All right,' Ygenio said. 'We will get ready. Do you wish me to help you look for Rusty?'

'No. No, I'll do that alone,' Clay said. 'You got to get Apolinaria out of here. There ain't the time for you comin' up there with me. You better get the horses saddled right away.'

Apolinaria was staring into the darkness beyond the door of the house as though she was trying to absorb it all; but when Clay said this she turned and looked at him.

'Horses? What of the wagon? You mean I am to ride on a horse?'

Clay was very gentle with her. 'No time, Apolinaria; you got to go. You'd never make it in the wagon. You may have to travel fast.'

Apolinaria's eyes became liquid suddenly,

as she began to understand it, and she stepped away from Clay, as though calling on some inner spirit of defiance.

'On a horse,' she said quietly. 'On a horse I must ride from this place; a *caballo. Madre de Dios!'*

When Ygenio ran off to the corral Clay went inside the house to get such things as he might need and could fit into his saddlebags. Already the interior had a deserted feeling for him, in much the same sense that the dooryard had the aspect of being seen from memory. He tried to speed his packing up, to close that odd sensation out of him, but it persisted and everything he touched and looked upon acquired the feel and appearance of the dry disintegration of antiquity.

Beyond the wall partition which separated his room from that which Apolinaria and Ygenio occupied, he heard the muted movements of her packing. He remembered that she had occupied that room for nearly as long as he could recollect and he didn't like to contemplate the thoughts that must be going through her head. He remained in his room until the sounds from the other had faded out and it was still again.

Apolinaria was seated on the gentle buckskin mare when Clay came outside. She had changed to her most voluminous skirt, and except for her tenacious grip upon the horn one might have thought that she was riding sidesaddle. She was completely cloaked in fallen folds, yet notwithstanding this she had draped the old rebozo in such a way that its fringes hung below the leather points of the tapaderos. Ygenio was on the ground beside her, tightening up the cinch.

'We are ready,' he said to Clay. 'We will go now. Are you certain I cannot help you?'

'Yes,' Clay said. 'That's all right. You go ahead. Did you turn the remuda out?'

'Yes,' Ygenio said and he gathered the reins of his own horse, steadied himself, and lifted up. 'I turn them out. I hope they run far.'

'Likely won't, but we might as well make it as tough for them comin' up as we can. Good luck. I'll see you.'

'Yes,' Ygenio said. 'Good luck.'

Clay watched them move away. He wondered if Apolinaria might have a parting word, but she did not; but her face was sufficiently eloquent to make any words unnecessary. It was like Abrana sitting in the stage again, and he wondered if all women were that way in leaving something that meant much to them. Keeping it all dammed up inside like that.

He waited in the dooryard until Ygenio and Apolinaria were becoming anonymous motion in the shadows of the trees. Then he went inside again. What time was left he wanted for himself.

He felt like a ghost walking through those

lonesome rooms. He kept remembering the early days, and while they had been hard they had been happy and satisfying, too. Until the Lincoln fight there had been a kind of peace and happiness about it all. Hardin and his ma had known they were building good and building for the future. They'd worked hard and long, but that had never seemed to bother them. His ma had always said that the length of a person's life never mattered as much as the manner in which he spent his allotted time. She had lived that way, and so had Hardin. And they had built this place and left it in his care.

It made him wonder if he was doing the right thing in going off again and leaving it. It made him think that he maybe ought to hole up here with his guns and what food there was, and let them come and drag him out. It would likely be a noble thing to do.

But he had a notion that Hardin and his ma would not approve of that. A thing like that was too deeply rooted in instinct, and a wise man would go off somewhere and bide his time. A wise man knew when the odds were too great to be worthy of consideration. He never got anywhere by being impetuous and losing his head, and maybe his life, in some vainglorious action.

He took his leave of the place in a little while. He left everything as it had always been and he took the roan horse around the corral and across the grassland to the north. A quarter of a mile beyond he came upon the remuda, which Ygenio had turned out to forage for itself, and as he passed among the horses some of them would lift their heads and look at him. In their own way, they likely wondered, too.

As he went higher he could look back and see everything dozing in the sun, quiet and oddly lifeless, like one of those abandoned Indian pueblos melting in the earth through centuries of time. There was a silent, lonely peace about it all and it seemed like nothing bad or unsettling could ever happen to that place, and yet it was happening. A man could never know what fate might overtake him from one moment to the next. It made him sour and bitter, and he swore at everything.

He took his time going along the high ground back there. He wanted to find Rusty and get heading for the hills, but he had to see the end of it as well.

He was fairly high above the place when the long spine of dust came winding up the valley from the town. He could only see the twisting ribbon of it in the beginning, but it came onward in a hurry, rising and falling, following the contour of the stage road. When it turned into the alley he felt the apprehension gnawing at him. The men in that posse were angry men and there was likely no accounting for their actions. He kept thinking that they might devastate the place, or even burn it to the ground. He kept hoping there were sober minds as well.

It seemed damned peculiar sitting up there like that, watching those men riding into his dooryard, stomping on his gallery and pushing through the doors into his home, and him not daring to show his nose or lift a finger to prevent whatever it might be that they were going to do. Just seeing them do that little bit drove a goad into him, made a voice shout inside him to go on down again and drive them out, or perish in the trying.

But he simply waited there and watched it all.

The afternoon was burning dusky when he saw the first light shining soft through the window of one of the darker rooms, and an involuntary sigh went out of him. He knew it was all right now. Men bent on arson and destruction did not pause to light a lamp. They were not going to fire it, at least. There would likely be some of them staying on a while to see if he was coming back or not, but the place would stand. He was sure of that.

When part of the group emerged from the house and went like shadows down the alley and back toward town he got back on the roan and headed north again. A little ways up he passed the place where he'd seen Rusty that day, and a bit beyond that the one where Diamond-Back had lain with his rifle in the grass—Rusty had shown him that. Turning west, he rode toward the barranca where Rusty had found the tracks of the Gallaghers' stolen stock. Remembering those things now, it seemed that a great stretch of time had intervened between those incidents and this, but he knew it hadn't. It was just a few weeks, a couple of months, and everything was ended.

Near the lip of the barranca he found Rusty's horse. He didn't see it right away because it was grazing over behind a growth of yucca and he was nearly upon it before he realized its presence. He dismounted and approached the animal with wariness, though he could not think exactly why. He was thinking that it was a good horse and that Rusty had always taken care of it. He was thinking that this affection had been returned in kind and that the animal rarely left the vicinity where Rusty might be. He had a sick apprehension in his middle because of knowing this.

When he neared the horse it looked up, made a small whinny, then went on grazing. Clay took hold of the bridle and ran his hands along the neck and flanks, looking for some kind of clue or other. Coming around in back of it he was on the edge of the barranca, and he looked down. There was still life enough in the sun to cast the alkali's reflection into his eyes. It made Rusty's body look miragelike,

153

suspended in the waves of dying heat. It made it look like it was still vibrant with life and being, but he knew it wasn't. The hot sun had already caused the blood to crust and dry about the wide wound channel between Rusty's shoulders. Clay did not have to go down in there to know that Rusty was dead.

He stood looking down at Rusty, absorbing it, and then, without any thought about it he turned his head and looked at the far-off mountains, humped cripples crouching in the failing light. Somewhere in those mountains Robey Moore was likely waiting, his mind was telling him. In his own way Moore'd been right about nearly everything, he was thinking. Robey'd one time said he'd get him back, and now it seemed he would.

Only maybe in a way he hadn't thought of. One of them would never leave those mountains. There was no other way any more. No other way at all.

12

He buried Rusty Rhodes in a shallow grave, heaping rocks upon the mound to keep the varmints out. The ground was hard and crusted, beaten and baked by milleniums of sun, and it was difficult to work without the proper tools. He found a small and natural depression in the ground, and after hacking at the sides with slabs of stone, and smoothing here and there with his rifle butt he got it to required size, and laid Rusty into it. It occurred to him he might make good use of some of Rusty's equipment, but when he thought about it the idea became indecent for him, and he buried him with everything.

With his rifle lying at his side, the muzzle just beneath his ear, Rusty looked something like a soldier sleeping at attention.

When he was through with that he stripped the horse and turned it loose. He didn't want to dig another hole and so he hunted in the barranca until he found a cavity of a size to hold the saddle and the bridle. Then he filled the rest of it with stones, and hoped they would keep the coyotes and the other animals from the leather; until he could get back and dig it up again.

After that was done he started west. It was getting on to dark, and because Apolinaria and Ygenio must have stretched their lead on him by quite a bit he wouldn't strain himself to try and catch them. It didn't make much difference if he rode with them or not as long as he knew where they were heading for. And he had enough gear along with him to spend the one night in the open. Anyway, he would like to be alone a while; he'd like to get things sorted out, and solitude might help in that direction.

He kept along the Hondo, heading toward the Capitans. He'd never thought he'd be entering these hills again for such a purpose, but he was doing it. His destiny seemed as deeply rooted in their ancient soil as the pine and cedar and aspen bursting from their flanks. Nearly every guiding force in his young life had had its inception in those mountains. A special kind of fate seemed to beckon to him from up in there. A malevolent sort of magnetism seemed to draw him toward those round and purple bosoms.

His mind kept turning back to the last time he'd ventured into these mountains from the valley. His mind kept turning back to that long-gone time and he remembered how he'd gone back home again after the last fight he'd taken part in—at Blazer's Mill; and how he'd tried to take up ranching once again. He recalled how he'd been busted up with Robey and the bunch, and how his freedom had turned into a lost feeling where everything was indefinite and without purpose. How he was at loose ends because he knew the Lincoln fighting wasn't ended just because he'd gotten out of it.

Ygenio and Apolinaria had been very patient and careful with him in those days and weeks, but a day had come when the drag upon him from the hills had been too much to bear. He remembered now how he had gone back up upon that day; and what had happened all because of it.

*   *   *

The day he got to Lincoln was a fine one, he remembered that. It was bright and clear and the town was lazing in the warm July sun. Lincoln lay against a steep uprising of the Bonito canyon and the old adobe and timber buildings lay lumped in comfort along the road and creek; Murphy's Big Store, the Torreon, the Ellis House, the McSween-Tunstall store and bank, the San Juan church. The air was soft and gentle with the quiet mountain breezes. Bright flowers made spots of color against the brown and golden building mud and plaster. The Bonito murmured a tune in drowsy passing. Birds flitted in the trees. There were people moving back and forth, and others lounged around the building stoops.

It did not have the look of a place that had been lately ripped and torn by gunfire.

But if the day was good his choice of time was not. The people in that town were as sore and angry as a hive of badgered hornets. Since he had felt compelled to return to that country he could have picked a better time. He had got there only shortly after the final battle of the war. The engagement had occurred within the town itself, and local spirit and temper were shaken to their core.

157

Murphy and McSween, the organizing leaders, were dead and buried, but the town was seething still. The hired killers had departed for the hills, and the brutalized village folk were in the market for a scapegoat for the violations of those men. Clay could have picked a better time, all right.

But all unknowing, he tied his horse to the hitch-rack before the Ellis House and walked slowly along the street. The McSween home was lying in charred and tumbled ruins and the sight of it induced a creepy feeling up his back. He knew something big had happened. When he was back at the Ellis House again, an old man rocking on the gallery told him what had come to pass. This old guy did not appear to recognize him, and he gave freely of what he'd seen and heard.

'I'll tell you, sonny, if'n it's fightin' a body likes then that body should have been here four days back. There was surely enough of it to suit most anyone.'

Clay had this jumpy, nervous feeling in him now and he was careful to keep his face beneath the shadow of his hat. Already, he was beginning to think himself a fool for wishing to get back into it again; he was beginning to think it was a stupid thing to come back up here as he'd done. Why in hell, he wondered, hadn't he stayed down at the ranch where he belonged? He had his belly full of fighting, he'd made his break; why didn't he leave well enough alone?

'I seen that building that got burned down over there,' he said to the old guy rocking in his chair. 'Was there fightin' in it?'

'There surely was. Right in there and all around it.' The old man slid a squinting sidewise glance at Clay. 'That there place is what's left of Alex McSween's house; ain't you been up here before?'

Clay was conscious of the rheumy, watery eyes picking at his face and body, and he lied as casually as he could.

'No,' he said. 'I ain't been up this way before. Just now more or less goin' through. To Carrizozo, lookin' for a job. Carrizozo, that's where I'm headin' for.'

The old man leaned back into his chair again. He took a bite of plug and some of the juice flowed mustard-yellow in his whiskers. 'Well, that's where it was, all right. McSween holed up in there with his wife and a bunch of others. He had this Jim French in there and Doc Skurlock, Tom O'Folliard and this Billy Bonney—oh, a lot of 'em, he had—and they all fought it out with Murphy's bunch. Even the Fort Stanton troopers was in it for a spell.'

'The hell you say,' Clay said to him. He tried to think it out; it must have been a battle royal.

'Yup, they was in it, all right. Didn't do no shootin', though. Didn't have to. Feller named Chavez brung up nigh a hundred greasers to

159

side McSween, and Colonel Dudley of the troopers got his Gatlings down here and said did one greaser pull a trigger the troopers would go into action. I tell you it was shaping up to something. But Chavez took the hint and got his outfit out of there. Some thought Dudley was acting in the public interest to keep the size of the fighting down, but others said he and Murphy'd one time served together, and that he was in cahoots with Murphy's men. Can't prove nothin' by me, except that once Chavez left it was only a matter of time.'

Clay stared at the charred ruination of McSween's home. He was trying to reconstruct its demolition. He remembered that Murphy'd had connections at the Fort, that he'd had that beef contract. 'Was it the troopers that burned it down?' he said.

'Nope. They just kind of stood around and watched, to keep the fightin' from spreadin' out, the Colonel said. It was during this palaver between Dudley and the opposing parties'—the old guy savored the sound of the phrase—'that the fire started. Murphy's crowd took care of that; I mean the crowd that worked for him—him bein' dead from sickness just a bit. But they set her afire and when she got to goin' good them inside was forced to make a break. I was lookin' out a window in the church and I seen everything. I could hear the firin', and every now and then

I'd hear McSween's old lady playin' her piano; figure that out! Bangin' it like crazy as the flames was risin 'round her. Then all at once they come pourin' out like rats. It was night by then, and everything looked bloody with the fire, and there was so much shootin' it sounded like an avalanche.'

'I'll be damned,' Clay said. He could see it vividly. He could see the flaming house and hear the weird crescendo of the woman's playing and the roar of gunfire as the men poured through the door. He could see them running blindly, stumbling and falling as the bullets pulled them down. 'Who was hit?'

'A lot of 'em was hit. On both sides, but mostly on McSween's. Yessir, a lot went to their Maker in that hour. McSween was the first to go. They was waitin' for him in particular, and when he went down just outside the door he was weighin' maybe twenty pounds more'n normal; from the lead, of course. And you know? He didn't even have a gun. Just a Bible in his hand. Funny kind of feller.'

The old guy paused at this point, staring blankly at the ruins, and it was clear to Clay that McSween's behavior in this extremity was incomprehensible to him.

'A Bible,' the old guy said again; and then his jaws resumed the movement on the cud. 'Well, after McSween, Harvey Morris went down, and then a couple of Mexicans. On

161

Murphy's side, Bob Beckwith got it; he was killed. And a couple of others wounded. Billy the Kid done most of that damage, and he got away with his crowd in the dark.'

By God, Clay thought; it was just coming over him. Murphy dead. McSween dead. The Lincoln war was over. No reason for hired gun hands now, and they sure wouldn't stay without bein' paid. By God, he could go on back for certain now. He could go on back and never leave again.

He tried to keep this excitement out of his voice and manner as he asked another question. He had to know about this one more thing.

'I didn't hear you mention Robey Moore,' he said. 'I don't suppose his bunch was in that one.'

The old guy was quiet for a moment and Clay felt a tight thing get into his throat and neck. The rheumy, watery eyes were sliding around toward him again, with a far-off remembrance creeping into them. The old man's voice got careful.

'Moore? No, I don't remember he was in it, though he's known to be around here somewhere. Folks figure he was startin' to run beef aside of the fighting.'

The old man was looking squarely at Clay now, his mouth dipped slightly open so Clay could see the rotted stumps of teeth, and the tobacco plug nestling in amongst them.

'What'd you say your name was, sonny?'

'I don't guess I did,' Clay said. He pulled at his hat. He hitched at his belt, nodded at the old guy and walked toward the steps leading to the road. Gawdalmighty, what a fool he'd been! Bringing Robey's name into it like that. Gettin' that old gossip's mind off along another track. He could feel the old guy's eyes boring into him, suspicious now, maybe dead certain. It made him walk fast, stiff. Then the voice sliced between his shoulders, shrill, filling the sleepy road with sound.

'Hey! I know you! You rode with Moore! I see you in this country before. God damn it, you're that Forrest kid!'

Clay kept on going straight ahead. He wanted to break and run, but he held back. All them people looking at him now. All them stupid, staring people, and where in hell had they all come from anyway? They surely hadn't been out there before, or hadn't seemed so anyway. It sure was queer how a street filled up when you least expected it. He had to get away from them. He had to get around a corner somehow; get out of sight, then double back and get his horse and then get out of town. My God, what a fool he'd been!

A pair of young girls turned at the sudden sound of the old man's cries, stared with fear, then added their screams to his shrill piping. A brown-faced washerwoman with a basket on her head flapped across the street in front of Clay like a chicken. The basket heeled and toppled, streaming laundry in the road. All around him folks were yelling now, and pointing at him, running.

He got around the corner of the Ellis House and slunk along the side of it and to the rear. The cry was a goddamned chant behind him now. He could hear it everywhere. They had the scent and they had to have the kill. He kept on going.

He came around the rear of it and headed toward the other side. There was a lot of racket behind him and he knew he had to hurry. An ax of panic was hacking at his nerves, and he got careless once again. He turned the corner, not scouting first, and nearly ran Dad Peppin down; Dad Peppin, he remembered suddenly, sheriff after Brady had been killed, ex-Murphy man to boot. Clay saw the big star, and stood there. Peppin's eyes bulged foolishly and he halted stock-still, afraid to draw.

Clay could have killed him and he knew it. He could have killed him and got out and maybe clean away, but something held him back from this. He had no record of any kind in that place that could be held against him. He'd been no hired gunslick in the fighting; his warring had been from conscience and conviction. All this sang through his head in those few seconds while Dad Peppin's eyes popped out at him in their astonishment.

Slowly, Dad Peppin licked his lips. 'Well, Forrest, what you goin' to do? You're pretty well surrounded.'

Clay kept his hands low and his shoulders hunched ahead. He knew how an animal at bay must feel. He knew Peppin recognized this, too, and was afraid of him because of it. 'Depends on what you want me for,' he said. 'I ain't done nothin' here. I didn't come up here for trouble.'

'Maybe. Maybe not,' Dad Peppin said. 'The people in this town ain't sure, though. They want to know. They've had enough of killin'. Your old bunch is raisin' hell, still, even though the fighting's ended, and the people will want to know what you're doin' here.'

'I ain't been with Moore for a good long while; I quit the fighting in the spring, been on my ranch since that time. You want to talk about it?'

'Might be best to do that,' Dad Peppin said carefully. 'You may be clear. You want to come along?'

Clay thought it over. The chase was coming around the far side of the Ellis House. It wouldn't be long now and he'd have real trouble. He'd wasted time here, and he'd have to do his talking with his gun, then. He had to make up his mind about this business quick.

'All right,' he said. 'I'll go with you. I'm clear on everything.'

165

So he went. He went with Dad Peppin, and the sheriff took him over to the Big Store, which was being used for such things now that Murphy was dead and the war was over. They locked him up in that place and three days later they rigged a charge against him.

For the murder of a man he'd never seen. With a name he'd never heard before.

*   *   *

Coming into the hills again after three years and more brought that all back into his head and made it fresh and green. He'd always been good about remembering details—Hardin had taught him the tricks of that in the hills and forests—and he could remember everything there was about the day they got him and the days that followed in the House, the Big Store, up at Lincoln; the trial, the judge batting away at flies all the time and hardly listening to what was being said; the perjured testimony of a runny-nosed witness which pinned this killing on him—testimony that was admitted as evidence regardless of its being circumstantial and the witness a known thief.

But that was enough. That's all they had to have—the form of it, mockery of justice or otherwise. That's all they wanted. They'd caught a man associated with those others who'd made such havoc in their town, and

166

they were going to take their anger out on him. It didn't make much difference how they fixed it up. Three years, they said to him. Three years, and they'd make it more if he'd been seen to pull the trigger, but they couldn't bring this boughten witness to go that far. But he'd gone far enough, the way that Clay looked at it; and he always wondered who had paid that man, and why.

Well, that's the way it was, and coming on up to these knowing hills again brought it all out for him to examine once again. Brought it all out and he could wonder how it happened.

But thinking on that business now didn't have any bearing on the present. These things didn't have much to do with what he was getting set for now. Stirring up his feelings with these old memories wasn't going to keep him calm and cool for Robey Moore.

On the second evening he went through Hondo in the hill and forest country. Ygenio had said his kinfolk were along the Lincoln road beyond that town and Clay figured Ygenio and Apolinaria would be there by now. Some distance out he came upon a cluster of 'dobes, a pole corral and a garden patch that seemed to fill the description Ygenio had given him. He got down from his horse and led him over that way from the road.

It was a cool and quiet night and the sounds from the *casas* carried far. He was wary of poking around in another man's property after dark and he strained his ears to hear a voice that he might recognize. He got in close beside a wall but he heard nothing that seemed to be familiar.

Then he turned around and saw the figure in the starlight. It was standing there behind him, and must have been there all along, beside a bush. He got scared and angry all at once, and then he heard the gentle laughter.

'Clay?' the voice said.

'Yes,' Clay said. 'It's me, Ygenio.'

'I wait for you here, outside. *Caray*, you are long in coming. I wait forever, I think.'

They were standing fifteen feet apart in the starlight looking at each other. There was a crazy quality about it, like each was from a different world.

'Yeah, I know. I got held up. I had to bury Rusty.'

'Rusty?' Ygenio's voice was very clear. 'Bury him?'

'Yes. I found him up there. Up there where he'd gone to look around. I guess someone was up there after all. Rusty didn't have a chance.'

13

After Ygenio turned Clay's horse into the corral he led Clay to a small clear place to the side of the largest *casa*, where a fire had been burning and had been allowed to die. While Ygenio got more piñon logs and brushwood with which to rejuvenate the blaze, Clay placed his saddle on the ground and arranged his blanket next to it.

'Do you wish to sleep here?' Ygenio said to him presently. The first flames were making headway with hesitation, and Ygenio was fanning them with a slow motion of his hand.

'I guess I might as well,' Clay said. 'I don't like to disturb anyone inside. It'll be all right out here. If it gets cold there's always the fire.'

'Yes,' Ygenio said. 'But you do not have to. There is plenty of room inside. Raphael would not want you to be uncomfortable. He would sleep out here himself, and think nothing of it, if he thought you would like it better in the *casa*.'

'No,' Clay said. 'There's no need for that. This is all right. I'll get along all right. I like it out here.' Which was true. He did not enjoy sleeping inside when he was away from the ranch. In strange places, he found it better for his peace of mind to have some room around him. He knew it was a throwback to the fighting days, but still it was no good to be closed in where he would have no place to go, but only stumble in the darkness, if he was called to move with haste. The time spent previously in these hills had conditioned him to that idea, and he was used to it.

'So,' Ygenio said. 'All right, then. It is for you to say. As long as you know that you may sleep inside, that is all.'

'This will be fine right here,' Clay said again.

He sat down on the blanket and Ygenio continued with the fire. It no longer required attention, but Clay recognized that Ygenio was keeping busy with it because he was reticent about speaking of Rusty and what had happened in the valley when the riders came from town. Then, as the flames burned fiercely, Ygenio sat back on his haunches and rolled a cigarette. When Clay rolled one, too, Ygenio lit them both with a burning stick.

'Did they damage it?' Ygenio said then, referring now for the first time to the ranch.

'No,' Clay said. 'I was where I could see, and I didn't see any damage done. They just rode in and walked around, then some went back to town. But the rest stayed, and I guess they'll have someone there 'til I go back again.'

'Ah,' Ygenio said. 'And when will that be? Will we go down soon?'

'No. Not yet. I got some things to do first.

There ain't no sense in going back until I clean up the basic cause of it all. I don't know—I might be able to square myself with all those people, but then it'd only start again. Anyway, there's Rusty.'

Ygenio was quiet while he thought about it. He was squatting on his haunches and his hands were cupped in front of him, with the cigarette between his fingers. The smoke went up in graceful deviations, and from time to time his eyes would follow it.

'Of course,' Ygenio said. 'I understand that. Do you know where to find this basic cause, as you call it?' Ygenio was being very formal with his language.

'I think so,' Clay said. 'I ain't positive, but I think I can find out pretty well.'

'Then it is very simple,' Ygenio said when Clay explained this. 'We will go to that place and do what is required, and then go home again.'

Clay did not say anything immediately. He was thinking that he didn't want Ygenio mixed up in this, but he knew that Ygenio would demand the right to participate.

'I'd better go alone and do this,' he said. 'These are bad men, and they stop at nothing. You know that.'

'*Por supuesto*, of course,' Ygenio said. 'I know that well. So—two of us will be better.'

'No,' Clay said to him. 'You don't know this kind. They're bad all the way through.'

171

'Well, I have known men of that sort before,' Ygenio said. 'I am not afraid. It makes no difference how bad.'

'I didn't say you were afraid. I just said they're bad. They're the worst there is. Outlaws all the way. Nothin' means anything to them. They kill for the fun of it. In the back or any way. It don't make any difference.'

'I know that,' Ygenio said. 'How many are there?'

'Should be four now. Bob Fergus was killed.'

'Then I must surely come with you,' Ygenio said. 'You cannot do it alone. How can you hope to deal with four of those if they are as bad as that?'

Clay dropped his cigarette into the fire. 'What about Apolinaria?' he said. 'You can't go runnin' off and leavin' her. Suppose you get shot. Then what?'

Ygenio shrugged, and poked at the fire. 'It will be all right. Anyway, she will be happy here while we are gone away. All these mouths to cook for. Yes, she will be in paradise.'

'What the hell,' Clay said, 'what the hell. All right. Don't blame me when you're spittin' blood, though. I tried to save your hide, remember that.'

'*Si*, I remember. If I die I tell the *Dios* that you warn me; I tell him everything. He will be good to you for that. He will be very kind and

172

gentle with you.'

'Fine.' Clay said it with light mockery. 'That's fine.'

Then Ygenio rose from the fire and went to the largest *casa*, from which the sound of energetic talk was coming, and presently he returned again, with three men who followed him at a distance of a few feet.

Two were young and tall, with dark faces and darker hair and eyes, and they stood solemnly with the fire flickering on them while Ygenio introduced them as his younger cousins who grazed sheep in the nearby hills. The other was the relative, Raphael, who had thick gray hair, and who was solid on his feet and in his manner, and very old. When he shook hands with Clay he bid him welcome to his *casa*.

'Thank you very much,' Clay said to him. 'You are very kind to take us in like this.'

'No. You honor us by coming to this poor place,' the old Raphael said. 'Everything we have is yours. Do you intend to sleep here on the ground?'

'Yes,' Clay said. 'It is all right here. I will be leaving early and I don't like to disturb anyone.' He was conscious of speaking as formally now as Ygenio had been doing before.

'They wish to meet you,' Ygenio explained to Clay. 'When they learn how you have lost your place they wish to welcome you here and make you feel at home.'

'Yes,' the relative named Raphael said. 'This is your home now, as it is ours, and you may stay forever, if you wish. Everything will be done to make you comfortable.'

'Thank you,' Clay said again, and he could think of nothing else to say.

When they went away again Ygenio walked part way to the *casa* with them, and then returned to the fire. 'Now that they have met you they will argue for half the night. But they wanted to make you welcome first.'

Clay looked at him in surprise. 'Argue? What about? Me?'

'No,' Ygenio said. 'They argue about everything. They enjoy doing that as a pastime, and they do it without end; mostly it is politics. But they wanted to make you feel at home before they started in with it.'

Clay sat down again and moved the saddle further away so he could use it as a pillow. He rolled another cigarette and waited until Ygenio had put more pieces in the fire before he took a stick with which to light the shuck.

'I will leave you now,' Ygenio said as he straightened up. 'It is late, and except for those who stay up to talk, the others are all asleep. Will you be all right?'

'Yes,' Clay said. 'I'll be all right. There is plenty of wood, if it gets too cold.'

'I can bring another blanket for you,' Ygenio said. 'Would you like that?'

'No,' Clay said. 'This is all right. This is fine.'

'All right. I see you in the morning, then. I will have a surprise for you in the morning.'

Clay rolled into the blanket, folded his hat onto the saddle and put his head on it. He saw the sly slant to Ygenio's eyes when he looked at him. 'What's that, steak for breakfast?'

'No,' Ygenio said. His laugh was secretive. 'It is better than that. You could never guess it.'

After Ygenio went away Clay lay with his cigarette between his lips, and watched the faint stars overhead. As the fire died slowly by degrees they became more prominent and presently they were very large and close. The whole sky was not visible to him, because of the trees growing on all sides of him, but the open place where he was lying, and where the *casas* stood, made it clear above. The trees became a kind of cone, with the bright stars hanging in the apex of it.

They were brilliant and he was glad to be out here where he could see them. He hoped he had not made a bad impression upon old Raphael with his insistence that he sleep outside, but this was better.

Besides, there was now too much noise indoors. Ygenio's kinfolk were numerous and of all descriptions, and now that the men were arguing, all of them seemed to be awake by consequence. There were infants, and he

175

could hear them cry and fuss; and there were mothers or aunts or older sisters, who ministered to these very young and made more commotion doing so. And there were others in between, the not-so-young, who asked drowsy questions and would not go to sleep again.

And the men were drinking tequila and aguardiente and talking politics without cessation. The more they drank the more they talked and the louder and more vociferous they became with their many arguments. He could hear Raphael condemning every government that had ever existed in the experience of man on earth, and the cure to everything seemed endless revolution. Ygenio had told him that Raphael had learned to do fine silverwork from a Navaho, but that didn't make any difference when he was drinking and talking politics in the evening. He was a revolutionary then, and had nothing whatever to do with silverwork.

It made Clay wonder about the unhappiness of those like old Raphael. They always wanted something different, and when that was accomplished they wanted something different still. It made him wonder if such happiness as they did have was not derived from the strife and turmoil of their arguing and unhappiness. It was not a clear thought, and he went to sleep while trying to work it out.

He awoke suddenly. He awoke so suddenly that it seemed to him that he had never been asleep at all, because he was as wide awake as he might have been at noon. But it was night, still, and his eyes were open and staring straight above him at the stars, which were very luminous now, because the fire was very low and only embering.

Then he heard the voice again, slow and soft, insistent. 'Clay. Clay.'

He sat up slowly, all alive. 'Abrana.' He could see her.

She came into the faded halo of the embers from the darkness and knelt beside him, not shyly, nor daringly either, but naturally, and kissed him; and then laughed softly. She was being very feminine.

'They would not let me sleep in there,' she said. 'But I could not anyway. I could not sleep.'

Clay was all the way up now. He was on his knees, and without saying anything he took the blanket and put it around her shoulders. He was thinking that it was cold and that she only had that blanket jacket on, but he was also thinking that his mind was partially blanked out with the surprise of this, and that he had to keep his hands moving until he could collect his wits about him. When he'd stirred the fire up, and put more wood into it, he returned and sat beside her.

'It is you, isn't it? I thought I was dreamin'

177

for a minute.'

'Of course, it is me,' Abrana said. 'I am as real as you are. Did I frighten you? I did not know whether I should come out here to you that way or not.'

'You gave me a start, I guess,' he said. 'That's all. I sure wasn't expecting you. I thought you'd be in White Oaks. What you doin' here?'

Abrana pulled her knees up and held them against her with her arms. The fire was becoming brighter and as she talked to him he could see the soft curve of her lips and the gentle contour of her face, all of it outlined with a line of gold, given it by the fire.

'I did go to White Oaks. I agreed to that. But I could not stay there. I did not wish to give Apolinaria pain, but still I could not stay. So I returned. I set out toward Roswell, and then I stopped here to think some more,' and she laughed as she added this. 'I have been here before with Ygenio and Apolinaria and I needed to stop some place to make certain it was right what I was doing.'

'When did you get here?' Clay said to her.

'Last night,' Abrana said. 'And Ygenio and Apolinaria came late this afternoon. I was not surprised to see them. I knew I had done right in starting back, then.'

'Was Apolinaria angry to see you here? And to know you were going back?'

'No,' Abrana said. 'It is all right with her

now. She understands it. She will not fight it now.'

Clay thought about it before he spoke again. 'You must be Ygenio's surprise,' he said. 'He said there'd be one in the morning, and he must have meant you.'

'He did?' Abrana was being gently humorous again. Her head was turned toward him, one cheek resting on her knees and the other glowing like an apple from the light. Her small teeth were very white, and slightly parted with her smile. 'I wonder why he said morning. Perhaps he thought I was asleep.'

'You should have let me know about this sooner,' Clay said to her. 'You should've come out right away. How was I to know you were here? That Ygenio.' Then he laughed, because he felt good.

'I did not want to bother you,' Abrana said. 'I watched you through the window for a while and I could tell that you and Ygenio had trouble to discuss, and I did not wish to intrude in that.' She paused, looking at the fire, and when Clay did not fill in the pause she added, 'I did not see Rusty coming up with you.'

'He's dead,' Clay said. 'He was shot.' He did not embellish it.

'He had nice stories,' Abrana said in a little while. She was still staring at the fire. 'He was very young.'

Then she turned around and looked at him.

179

'Is that why you have come up here? To see about that?' She was careful in her choice of words.

'Partly,' Clay said. 'We were run out anyway, but it's partly that.'

'Yes, Apolinaria told me of the other. She told me of it when they came this afternoon. Where will you go now?'

'I don't know for sure. There's a place near Encinosa that I'll try first. It's just a guess.'

'Will you go alone?' Abrana said. 'You should not go into a thing like that alone.' Her voice was very small.

'Ygenio wants to come along,' Clay said. 'I told him I didn't want him to, but he's coming anyway. He's too old for a thing like that, but he won't listen to sense.'

'He is not so old,' Abrana said. 'And he is very good and quick. He will be good to have with you. When do you go?'

'In the morning. There's no sense in putting it off. We'll leave early.'

She was looking at him again. She was looking at him and they were close together, and he put his arm around her shoulder and pulled her closer and kissed her warm and smooth. But it was awkward that way, so he took his arm away and lay back and put his head on his rumpled hat upon the saddle. Then he reached and pulled her toward him gently, until her head was resting in the crook his elbow made. She was quiet as they did this, and he arranged the blanket so that it folded over both of them.

Then he kissed her again and he could feel her body hard and tight against him as they held to one another. Her lips were soft and slightly parted, and they had strength in them, but not abandon.

'Clay . . .' Abrana said.

'Don't talk,' Clay said. He sounded angry, but he wasn't.

'Clay,' she began again. 'Please. Be careful.'

'Yes,' Clay said 'Don't talk.'

14

The sky was rich with dawn when Clay awoke. He was alone there by the gray, bent ashes of the fire, and Abrana had gone away. He didn't know when she had done this, because he'd been tired beyond his knowledge and had not been disturbed when she had gone. He had slept very easily and deeply after she had come out to him in the night before.

There was no noise yet from the *casas* as he got up from the ground and worked the stiffness out of his limbs. He was thinking he was hungry and that the last few hours before sunrise had been cold ones, and that he was chilled. Because of the quiet inside the adobes he would make his own breakfast and not disturb anyone inside for food, though he knew that both Abrana and Apolinaria would be impatient with him because of it. But he had some beans and bacon, and he could make coffee with water from the well, and he might as well make use of those things.

When he rebuilt the fire from twigs and brushwood, and then threw in a butt of pine to give it body, he took a piece of soap and a towel from his saddlebags and went around to the rear of the largest *casa*, near the corral. As he washed his face and neck and arms he thought how cold the water was, and then as he dried himself he remembered that he hadn't shaved in three days and that he must surely look like hell.

Well, it didn't matter much now, and it certainly wouldn't make any difference to Robey and the bunch whether he came upon them with a stubble on his face or not. But still it was in his mind in a disturbing kind of way and he wished he had the time to take those whiskers off.

It was funny such a thought could plague him at this time. Maybe, because his mind was filled with the magnitude of what was coming, his subconscious was trying to divert him with these other things.

When he finished eating he took his cup and frying pan around to the well again and washed them in the bucket. The sun was higher now, and coming through the trees, and he could hear the sounds of life resuming in the *casas*. Pretty soon he could see the small and quizzical faces of the children looking through the windows at him, hear the older people bumping here and there in grogginess, and a little after that he heard the corn being ground upon a *metate*, and he thought that would be Apolinaria.

When Ygenio came out Clay already had the roan fed and saddled, and was waiting for him.

'Ho,' Ygenio said, 'you are ready so soon. You are surely eager for it.'

'Might as well get on with it,' Clay said. 'Can't do no good sittin' around. Did you eat something?' Now that he was ready he wanted to get going. He didn't want to sit around. Especially, he didn't want to get involved with Abrana or Apolinaria, though he sensed they would not trouble him.

'All right, we go,' Ygenio said. 'I will eat something on the way. I will bring some jerky and some corn. Will you want some coffee, too?'

'I've got coffee,' Clay said. 'And bacon. We'll have enough. You still got time to reconsider this. You better think about it.'

'I am too old to think about it,' Ygenio said. 'I already make my mind up, and it is tiring to think of changing it.'

'All right,' Clay said. 'Let's get going then.' He was feeling tight inside now.

183

But Ygenio did not move off. 'I forget,' he said. 'You should have your surprise before we go. Abrana is here.'

'Is she now?' Clay said, and laughed. 'I found out last night.'

'Oh ho! Did you? What a sly one.'

'You couldn't keep a thing like that from me,' Clay said. 'You ought to know better.'

Ygenio buttoned the top button of his shirt, and rolled his sleeves down. 'Perhaps not. I simply wished you to have a good night's rest. I knew you would need it. Besides, I thought she was asleep.'

'Sleep ain't always so important,' Clay said. Then he looked around. 'Come on, let's get on with it.'

Ygenio went around to the rear of the *casa* to the corral, and Clay swung up on the roan and sat there, waiting for him. Ygenio's kinfolk were coming from the *casas*, now, and regarding him with large and quiet eyes. It occurred to him that they must know what he had come for; they had likely known it all along. He knew Abrana had not told them, and he didn't think Ygenio had either, but still they seemed to know.

These people were like that, he thought. They had a sense for death and trouble; like Ygenio and Apolinaria had had the day he'd killed the drunk in town. They had a nose for death stalking round about.

When Ygenio returned he removed his

184

sombrero and bowed to all of them. '*Adiós,*' he said. 'We see you soon.'

They stood there watching them. The old Raphael came through the doorway and bowed to them in return. The early sun made the gray in his hair shine like the fine filagree of silver which he worked, and he inclined his head with dignity. He did not look like a revolutionary now. Not far from him Abrana stood silently with her hands clasped across her narrow waist, and her eyes motionless on Clay. He could feel them like a physical caress.

'May success attend you, and may the good *Dios* ride at your side.' The old Raphael spoke with careful articulation.

'Yes,' Abrana said in a low tone. '*Vaya con Dios.*'

'*Gracias,*' Clay and Ygenio said together.

The others said nothing, but simply watched, and Clay's eyes went from Abrana to Apolinaria. She was standing a little apart from the rest of them and he wondered how a person so round and shapeless could in one particular moment become as straight and magnificent as she had now. There was the strength and ageless knowledge of the mountains in her face.

'And may the *Madre* guard and keep you,' she said to them.

And that was all. They rode away from the *casas* toward the road. Clay did not look back, though he badly wished to. It was very quiet all around them, and each hoof made a clear, distinct sound as it was placed upon the ground.

*　　　*　　　*

They rode west by north and the day was beautiful. They kept the Hondo on their left and made the beginning of an arc to take them around Lincoln without going through it. Clay had nothing to fear in that town any more, but he didn't want to be seen in that vicinity. There was always the chance of a stray word of warning getting on to Robey, wherever he might be, and he knew they'd need all the secrecy they could get. So they kept off the main roads and held to those trails little used.

For a long while they didn't say much, and went along in silence. Clay was thinking of a great many diverse things and he knew that Ygenio must be doing likewise. A man did not easily venture out to court his own destruction; he always had some thoughts about it. It didn't make much difference what kind of person he'd been before that moment. There came a time when he had to think those things out privately. He had to get into a certain frame of mind.

After a time he told Ygenio where they were heading for. He felt sure in his own mind

186

that Robey and the bunch would have struck for the high ground after the killing of Rusty and the latest depredations in the valley, and Ygenio ought to know about his reasoning on that.

'In the old days, after trouble, they'd go off and lie low for a while,' he said. 'They used to get off in the timber somewhere and sit around. Split up, even, for a time. I figure that's what they're doin' now. Like as not they got me into as big a jam as they can right now figure out, and they're goin' to see what happens.'

Ygenio considered it for a moment without saying anything. 'You think they know about that one in town? The one with whom you fight?'

'I don't know,' Clay said. 'Maybe. It wouldn't surprise me none if they did. Robey always seemed to know about what he ought to know, good or bad. He likely does.'

'You think, then, they are up there? *Mas alla*?' Ygenio waved his arm at the splendid trees and mountains.

'Yeah; I been thinkin'. I figure if we can find Steve Howard we can find 'em all. And I got a notion where we might pick him up. He used to keep company with a *mujer* up here not far from Encinosa. He used to spend a few days, more sometimes, up there after every bit of trouble. Seems to me it'd be natural for him to be up with her now.'

187

'Is that the one whose father has the sheep?' Ygenio asked. 'The one you tell me of whose sheep are killed?'

'No,' Clay said. 'That one's dead. That was Robey done that. This one ain't far from that place, though. Five, maybe ten, miles.'

'And you think that he will be at this place, this Howard—with the girl?'

'Can't say for sure, but it gives us something to go on. He was always weak for her in the old days.'

Ygenio laughed softly, and Clay looked at him with sudden self-consciousness, but he saw that Ygenio's mind was not on what he thought it was.

'That is a good one,' Ygenio said. 'A bad gunman who is weak for one of those. For the girls. I wonder how many times that has happened in the past. A gunman should keep his mind on business.'

'Yeah,' Clay said. 'But Steve's like that. That's why I figured we'd try him first. Maybe he won't be there at all, but if he is he'll talk. By God, how he'll talk.'

*   *   *

They kept going, but they took their time. Clay wanted to get to this place in the early evening and so they did not hurry. It was not much more than twenty miles or so between the *casas* of Ygenio's kinfolk and that of the *mujer* with whom Steve Howard sometimes kept company, and so there was no rush about it. It was simply a matter of proper timing and nothing else.

Toward mid-afternoon they commenced to ease down from the higher country once again. They'd stopped in Capitan Gap to brew some coffee and gnaw on Ygenio's jerky, and after that they worked through the backbone of the mountains and they were once more descending toward the foothills. There were aspen and pine and spruce upon the heights and cedar and piñon upon the lower trail they followed. Clay liked the aspen especially and admired the way in which the golden leaves were trembling and shaking in the air; their slim trunks like ivory columns. He wished he had the time and frame of mind just to sit there for a while and look at them.

It was shortly after nightfall when Clay saw the small light glimmering up ahead of them and he knew they had arrived. The place in which they were was familiar to him now, and he knew the light was shining from the *casa* of Howard's woman. How many times he'd ridden through this place before he could not readily recall, but he had done it frequently with Robey and the others. He remembered that Robey always had to come and get Steve away from her when it was time for them to be on the move again.

'All right,' Clay said. 'Here we are. We keep

quiet now. It's that light straight ahead up there.'

'I see it,' Ygenio said. Ygenio swung down from his horse before speaking to Clay again. 'Do we leave them here? This looks like a good place.'

'Yes,' Clay said. 'I guess we better. Stake 'em out is best. And no noise, now.'

'Yes, I will remember that. I will be very quiet. Like death, I will be quiet.'

'That may well be,' Clay said, and he squeezed Ygenio's arm.

They staked the horses in the cover and walked the remaining distance in a wary crouch. They circled the building once to get the lay of the land, and counted the horses in the small corral at the rear of the squat adobe house. There were two in there, Clay saw, and a frowzy-looking burro. All of them dozing, and not paying any heed.

At the front of the *casa* they stopped and lowered themselves behind some manzanita. Inside, Clay could hear the unexcited conversation and he didn't think that anything had been suspected. There was simply a placid drone, broken now and then by laughter and snatches of garbled singing.

Ygenio moved closer and cupped his hand against Clay's ear. 'Do we go right in?' he asked in a hoarse whisper.

'Maybe we better,' Clay said quietly. 'Anyway, we got to surprise 'em if we can.

190

Maybe we better bust right in.'

'Yes,' Ygenio said. 'Perhaps; but that would not be polite.'

Clay looked at Ygenio and saw him smiling. Ygenio's long mustachios had a humorous twist to them, which pleased him, because he knew that Ygenio felt good about what they were doing. Ygenio didn't always say too much about things of danger, but Clay knew he was the right one to have with him for a thing like this. Ygenio was always steady.

Easily, they headed for the door, then stopped again a few yards short of the low, wide stoop. 'You maybe better hang back here and watch them windows,' Clay said. 'No sense taking chances.'

'No, let us not take chances,' Ygenio said, and laughed silently into his mustachios. 'All right. I do that. I watch the windows very well.' Ygenio stopped talking and drew his gun. Clay had never paid it any heed before this time, but now he saw it was an old Colt with a heavy, ugly barrel. Ygenio smiled at Clay's silent appraisal of it.

'It is a good one,' Ygenio said. 'It is very good for mending fence, and it has a fine spring, too, for shooting. It is just right.'

Clay nodded and went up on the stoop. There was a kind of waiting quiet now and Clay had the fear that those inside had heard them talking. They must have made too damned much noise, he thought; then, directly

191

against the door he heard a body moving, then a voice.

'*Quién es?*' it said. '*Quién es?*'

Clay kept quiet. He crouched on the stoop, tight again inside, his gun clamped in his fingers. His breathing sounded like a high wind passing through his nose.

'Damn it,' someone else said. 'Sit down.' And Clay recognized Ed Picket's voice. That accounted for the second horse.

'I heard something,' the first one said, and because it was distinct this time Clay knew Steve Howard was the nearest one. 'I heard talkin' out there.'

'Perhaps it was the horses.' A girl's voice, light with banter. 'The burro, she is always talking; perhaps she was making conversation with your horses. Consuelo is very courteous with guests.'

Clay heard Steve Howard make a rude sound with his lips. Then the door opened and a thin slice of light cut across the stoop. Clay pressed against the dried mud and waited. When it opened further and Howard poked his head out, Clay swung the gun around and pushed it into Howard's belly.

'Hello, Steve,' he said.

Steve Howard stood there, rooted. His face looked loose, like an old shirt. His lips were moving, but no sound came.

Clay reached out with his other hand and got a grip on Howard's belt. He jerked him through the door and off the stoop, beyond the light. At the same time, Ed Picket swore, kicked the door shut and smashed the light out. The girl screamed, then whimpered as something struck her hard. Picket's fist, likely, Clay thought. Ed always was short on patience.

Clay kept his hold on Howard's belt until he got him out of line with the door and the windows on that side of the house. He knew that Howard was astonished and bewildered, but that it was wearing off. He saw that he was being wary of the gun, though.

'Damn you, Forrest, what in hell you think you're doin'?' Steve Howard said.

'I come up here to have a talk with you,' Clay said. 'I want to know where Robey might be found.'

Steve Howard was getting adjusted to it. 'You did, huh? Well, I don't know. And if I did I ain't so sure I'd let you in on it.'

Clay swung the gun in a fast arc and raked Howard's face with the heavy muzzle and the front sight. Steve Howard stumbled backward with the impact and Clay came up with the gun and raked the other side; he remembered the way he'd pistol-whipped the man who'd shot his father with the shotgun, but he felt different about this thing with Howard. He felt glad inside for doing this to Howard.

Everything was coming out of him and he felt glad and happy. He kept smashing at

Howard's face until the outlaw sank to his knees and groped blindly for Clay's legs, more in supplication than attack. His voice was hollow and far away and filled with bubbles.

'Forrest,' he said. 'Forrest, Jesus, Forrest.'

Clay hit him once more before he stopped. 'Where is he, Steve? Tell me where he is. That's what I want from you.'

Howard tried for Clay's legs again, but Clay stepped back. He felt like slugging him one more time for that, but he held his arm back.

'He'll kill me if I tell you, Clay; God, Forrest, you know how he is. He'll kill me if I tell. Just a couple weeks ago he killed Bob Fergus for no reason at all; hung him to a tree for Chrissakes. With his two hands—and for no reason; he's insane.' The words were all run together in the hollow bubbles.

'Robey done that, huh. All right. Anyway, he won't get to you, Steve. He'll never get near you.'

Steve Howard was on his hands and knees. His head hung low between his shoulders, and even in the starlight Clay could see the blood stream darkly, dripping on the ground beneath him.

'He's up on the Ruidoso,' Howard said. 'He's up there with Diamond-Back. They're stayin' up near Bowdre's old place. Up near where your pa was killed that time. They was goin' to pick us up again down here in four, five days, a week.'

Clay put his gun in the holster and his hands on his hips. He raised his head and looked around, taking a deep breath as though to cleanse his lungs of putrid air. It sure was beautiful out here tonight, he thought. These fall evenings were mighty pleasant in the hills.

'All right, Steve,' he said to Howard, 'you can get up now. You don't need to grovel around like that.'

Steve Howard raised his head and looked at Clay. His eyes were large and round, and haunted now by fear.

'What you goin' to do?'

'Get up,' Clay said to him. 'I said Robey'd never get near you and I mean to keep my word. I'm givin' you an even break, Steve. More'n you ever gave to anyone. More'n my man Rusty Rhodes got. Come on; get up.'

Steve Howard stared at him.

'Wait a minute! Listen, Clay, listen, you got me all wrong. Why, I had nothin' to do with that Rhodes kid; that was Diamond-Back, sure as hell. But, listen, look, it's Robey that's in back of everything; he's your man, Clay. For God's sake, Forrest, listen! Robey done everything to you! Everything! He even got you framed at Lincoln!'

Clay felt a stiff sharp thing get into his back. 'What?'

'God, yes! Nobody can get away from him. He swore he'd fix you when you put your gun

195

on him at Blazer's Mill. When he heard Peppin was holdin' you for a talk he got the notion of stickin' you with something. There'd been a card-game shooting a couple days before, and he bought this little no-account to say you done it. That's all Peppin an' the others needed. That town was hot, then. They was fed up with everything in that place. But that was just a starter; he figured to ride you to death and ruin when you got out from serving your time. He was never goin' to let you rest again.'

'That was it, huh?' Clay said, and he was aware of feeling ill as he thought of it. 'All right, Steve, thanks for everything.'

'Forrest! Listen!'

Clay waited for him. It happened as he thought it might. Howard moved slowly on his knees, then dropped and rolled. At the same time his gun whipped upward from his leg, and Clay heard the two guns fire in one report, felt the hot wind rush over him, and saw Howard sink down slow and flatten out. He hadn't been aware of firing, but he was holding his gun again, and there was Howard, shapeless on the earth.

Clay turned around and walked back toward the *casa*. When he passed the stoop he heard one more solitary shot, and that was all. Ygenio was standing at the corner of the building and Ed Picket lay halfway through the window on the other side, one arm dangling toward the ground, and his thick, long hair streaming down.

'He was curious,' Ygenio said. 'It was only time. I simply wait for him. The spring works very fine.'

Within the *casa*, Howard's *mujer* whimpered in soft spasms.

15

They went back through the timber of the Capitans, toward the Ruidoso over south. Clay had this weak-kneed nausea in him now, and there were times when he thought he was going to lean across his stirrup and maybe let it go. He wondered why in hell what they had done should affect him that way. He wondered why an extermination job of that sort should make his belly lose its equilibrium.

But then he knew it didn't make much difference who the dead men were—what the characters of those men might have been while living. Killing was killing, whatever the guise or attitude, and he could never achieve a mental approach which would make it seem impersonal to him. He could never be a Robey or a Diamond-Back.

But in another way he felt better, too. He had the feel of the necessity of what they had embarked upon and he was impatient to get it over with. He knew that what they'd set out to do was as inevitable as the rising and setting of the sun, and since he'd long accepted it in that light these other things didn't make much difference. His belly could kick up all it cared to, it was still going along on this thing until it all was finished; one way or the other.

They had to stop, though, on their way to Bowdre's old place. They needed food and rest if they were going to see this through. They couldn't plow along on nervous tension and this geared-up feeling for getting it over and done with. He couldn't be a fool about it. He knew he had to use his head.

Toward midnight they had passed back through the Gap and had reached a point on a quiet-moving stream a few miles to the west of Lincoln. It looked good enough to spend a few hours in, but most any place would have been all right with him, and he hardly felt his feet hit the ground when he dismounted. Unsaddling the roan and putting it on the picket rope was just like going through the motions. But he couldn't keep his mind from racing on when he was rolled in his blanket on the ground. The damned thing wouldn't slow down for anything.

'Here, you take some of this,' Ygenio said out of the darkness next to him.

'What's that?' Clay said, and then he felt the piece of jerky being pushed into his hand.

'You chew on that,' Ygenio said. 'You get

tired in a little while. It is good for your *estómago.*'

'I'm plenty tired now,' Clay said. 'I'm all right.'

'Well, you chew it anyway. Pretty soon your head aches with chewing and then you go to sleep.'

'My head's aching now,' Clay said. 'I'm one big ache all over.'

But he chewed on the jerky like Ygenio said for him to do and in a little while his mind stopped sizzling. It would make an excursion every now and then, but these got less frequent and pretty soon it was hanging right around where he could keep track of it. The last thing that he remembered was the long-gone trial in Lincoln and the judge batting at the flies and the little no-account telling how it was when he'd seen Clay standing over the murdered card player with his pistol in his hand. And himself trying to figure out who the no-account might be and what it was he was talking of, and why this thing was happening to him, and how. And now he finally knew. He went to sleep with that relaxing thought; he finally knew.

It was dawn when they were up and moving out again. Ygenio filled the coffee pot at the stream, tossed some bacon in the pan, and they each had some more of Ygenio's jerky to top it off. It had a nice taste, all of it, in the early morning air of the high country, but Clay didn't have an appetite. He didn't have an appetite and he didn't eat much because he was impatient about what was coming up, and because he had this tight thing in his belly once more. In a way it was much the same as he'd felt on the day he'd ridden out with Hardin, but in another way it wasn't. He was more sure of himself this time and he knew what was going to happen and what he was going to do. He would be on the giving end of it this time.

But the tight thing was there just the same, and he knew it likely always would be in a thing like this. It likely always would be when there was a shooting to be thought about.

Morning in the timber was always the most beautiful time of day, but Clay could not get over the seemingly sinister aspect of it. It had had that quality for him ever since the day that Hardin had been killed; but the fight at Blazer's Mill had impressed him with it even more. Very likely that was because the Buckshot Roberts thing had been foul and dirty, while the other had been natural and perhaps to be expected, or anyway, accepted, as a hazard to be taken. But it seemed to him that everything dark and bad had happened or begun in the morning in those forests. The beauty of the trees was deceptive in that way, he thought. They seemed to sing of peace and tranquility, but Clay could never forget how it had been that day when they went for

Buckshot Roberts.

They were full of ghosts, those woods. Much of the Lincoln fight had raged in there, where the slow hills flowed together, then lifted up again; where the trees were high and bearded and where the shadows of their branches and their bulk lay in lakes of blue and black along the ground. And the ghosts of those now dead and, by some, forgotten, like as not, seemed to glide on soundless, spectral hooves among those shadows once again.

Sometimes Clay would steal a glance at Ygenio as they went ahead. The trail would now and then widen out sufficiently for them to ride abreast, and sometimes when this would happen Clay would steal a look and wonder what was going through his mind. You could never tell what men like him were thinking, it occurred to Clay. You could never tell because they always seemed to be the same, no matter what they happened to be doing.

One time Ygenio noticed Clay's covert watching, and he reached across to Clay and slapped his knee.

'A fine day in the woods, yes?' he said. 'A fine day. Yes, a fine day for anything. How do you feel?'

'Why, I feel pretty good, I guess,' Clay said. 'How in hell do you feel?'

Ygenio laughed again and Clay wondered why men always inquired after one another's

201

health at a time like this. Why they were always going around and asking everybody how they were. Hardin had done it that day so long ago, and even Robey Moore himself had not been immune to it. Robey was always trying to find out how people felt.

'Me, I feel fine, too,' Ygenio said. 'It is all in the thinking, Clay, and I am just now thinking how fine I feel. I say to myself, I say, "Ygenio, you are going into the mountains this beautiful morning. You are going into the mountains to have a fight, and that may have some good in it; it is a fight which has perhaps been a great while in coming and it is right that you should go. When it is done you will go back to the ranch and sit under the trees and grow old. It is a very nice place for that purpose." '

'Yeah,' Clay said. 'That'll be a great thing, all right. We'll get this over with and go back and grow old.' And he laughed at the way he said it.

Well, maybe they would at that, and why should he laugh? Maybe they'd do just like Ygenio said they would, and what was there to stop them? Just saying it that way seemed to make it something more than merely possible. By God, it could happen like Ygenio said; they would do just that. They would finish with Robey and then go back and grow old beneath those trees. But Robey would come first. That devil. That horned bastard.

He kept wondering why he hadn't been particularly surprised when Steve Howard told him about Robey's hand in the trial at Lincoln. It was likely because it was the most natural thing in the world for Robey Moore to do. It was really a kind of credit to him in a way. It almost made Clay admire Robey's mental agility, a quality which had always been a thing of quiet amazement for him.

You never knew what to expect of Robey Moore, except that it would be original. His approach to a problem was always rare and imaginative. Like those sheep. It must have delighted him to have had a hand in that Lincoln trial; he likely savored rigging that a good deal. Likely broke into loud guffaws every time he thought about it. Kept him laughing a good three years, it had. Damn him, Clay thought. Damn him, damn him, damn him.

'Clay,' Ygenio said in a little while, and when Clay looked at him he saw this teasing humor that Ygenio would sometimes get in his face. 'I wonder.'

'What about?'

'Why, I wonder if you will marry with Abrana when we are finished with this.'

'You do?' Clay said. 'Do you think I should? Would you approve of that?'

Ygenio laughed with his head tipped slightly back. 'I would never try to give advice on such a thing. What difference if I approve or not? A man is a fool to ask another such a question. Marriage can be very personal at times.'

'Do tell,' Clay said. 'Well, does the idea of Abrana appeal to you? Or doesn't it?' Now that they had got around to it he wanted to know what Ygenio thought about it. It was something he'd been wondering about, and Ygenio's attitude was important to him.

'She is very nice,' Ygenio said with caution. 'She is surely competent in many ways.' Ygenio pressed his thumb upon the saddle horn. 'Perhaps you are better qualified to judge her on other matters.'

'Now, ain't you the smart one, now,' Clay said. 'You still ain't said, though. What about Apolinaria?' he added. That was important, too; maybe more important than Ygenio.

'Apolinaria? Oh, she would like it. She would have to adjust to it, but she would like it.'

'I thought she didn't like it. She was acting like I was a mortal enemy of hers, there, for a while.'

'I think she was afraid you did not know what you were doing. She was afraid for you, and Abrana, too. Now it will be different.'

'She come around, huh? Sure is funny, ain't it?'

'Ah,' Ygenio said, 'there you have grasped it. As long as you understand that you will be very happy.'

'Understand what?' Clay said. He wondered if Ygenio was leading him on.

'Simply that you will never understand,' Ygenio said. He squinted at the trees above the trail, and sighed. 'They are very complicated, the women of this world!'

* * *

Near noon they struck the Ruidoso and headed west again. They were very near to Charlie Bowdre's old place now. There wasn't much distance left to go; not much time left, either, as Clay figured it. They couldn't be but a couple of miles from Bowdre's spread.

The land around there looked familiar to him now. They'd ridden hell-bent through it the day that Hardin had gone down. If he looked carefully he'd likely find the place where the Murphy man had dumped the buck-load into him. Where Robey had knocked him—Clay—silly against the big pine bole.

He had to shut those things out of his mind. He couldn't have all those incidents in there cluttering up his thinking, getting in the way of the business coming up. His head had to be as straight and clear as a stretch of that Santa Fe railroad track. It had to be clean and open just like that.

When he heard the ax chucking through the trees he knew they'd got there. He couldn't see the layout yet, but they dismounted from their horses anyway. Not many men could do their best shooting from a horse, and they couldn't take a chance on a slip of that kind now. So they staked them out and walked forward through the trees. Ygenio slipped his gun out, then let it drop again, and smiled at Clay. Clay made sure the button on his right shirt sleeve was fastened proper. They kept going slowly through the trees. They kept a silence between each other as they walked along; there was nothing left to say. Glory, it was quiet up in there!

Coming into the clearing, Clay saw Robey standing near a woodpile with the ax. Robey had his sleeves rolled up and the muscles in his lower arms bulged from the way he held the ax. He held it just slightly off the ground as he watched them coming through the trees, like maybe he'd forgotten that he had it in his hands. Not far off, a few feet maybe, Diamond-Back paused with his cupped hands raised halfway to his face, the water dripping from them into the metal basin before him, on a wooden bench. Dawgoned funny to see Diamond-Back take the time and trouble to wash his face.

Clay stopped fifteen or twenty paces away, and waited. Ygenio stood a couple of yards to his right, his legs slightly spread and his hat tipped back as though he thought it might impede him otherwise. Diamond-Back wiped his hands slowly on a dirty cloth. Robey sank the ax into the end of a cedar butt, and rolled his sleeves down. Everyone knew what was going to happen.

'Hello, Forrest,' Robey said. 'Almost been expectin' you. Don't seem you changed much since I seen you last. Been nigh onto three years an' better, ain't it? How you feel, kid?'

Clay kept watching Robey Moore. You could never tell about him, he was thinking. His hands were hanging natural and easy around his belt line, his right hand dipped back a little, fingers partly curled. Diamond-Back was facing them directly now, his shirt wide open to his navel, and the matted hair on his chest glistening in the sun coming through the branches overhead.

'I feel pretty good, Robey,' Clay said. 'How about you?' There it was again.

Robey looked him over clinically. Robey's empty, vacant eyes drank him down and Clay commenced to feel the beginning of the strangeness he'd always had when Robey looked at him that way. Robey made a man feel more alone and solitary than anything on earth when he put his eyes on him like that.

'Looks like you kind of leaned out,' Robey said. They were still a good ways apart, but it didn't mean anything in that place. It was so still and quiet up in there that Clay could hear him perfectly.

'Yeah,' Clay said. 'Fellers do. Thanks to you I had time for it. I done most of it in jail.'

Robey smiled; with his lips he smiled at Clay. 'You finally figured that out, huh? Just a notion I had at the time, is all; wasn't much. Hearin' they was talkin' to you down at Lincoln gave me a chance I couldn't pass up. This guy I found didn't mind makin' a poke tellin' how he saw you with a pistol in your hand. Just enough time to make you think a while.'

'Steve Howard told me,' Clay said. 'I found him with his woman up near Encinosa. He told me a lot before he died.' Why in hell were they talking all this over anyway?

'Killed him, huh? Seems you changed quite a bit, kid. Didn't learn nothin' from that jail time, though, did you? Too bad; I had it figured to get you smartened up. Almost a waste for me to arrange it for you.'

'I smartened up enough, I guess. Enough to know you ain't goin' to push me around forever. I learned you ain't goin' to make me spend the rest of my life in hell.' He didn't feel anything. They were simply words.

'Sound like your old man when you talk like that; and look what it got him.'

'Ends for everybody some time, don't it?'

'Yah. Yah, you're right about that, kid. I had some choppin' to do, but it can wait. I been kind of lookin' forward to meeting up with you.'

Robey moved a pace or two from Diamond-Back. 'Any time, kid. Any time you say.'

Clay's ears picked up the forest sounds around them. Without thinking of it consciously, he heard a jay bird scatting somewhere in the pine boughs overhead. He heard a squirrel in argument farther off in the deep blue shadows; he heard the creek washing endlessly across the rocks. The slow wind rubbing the leaves and needles against one another in a soft and sighing undertone. Nothing ever changed up here, he thought. Nothing ever changed and it would be the same when that cabin, there, was rotten in the soil. When the small affairs of the men who'd built that place were dead in memory. Them same forest creatures, or their offspring, would be carrying on their timeless business just the same.

He heard Ygenio breathing next to him.

He kept watching Diamond-Back and Robey while these other things were coming into him. He kept watching them and waiting and he thought how Diamond-Back was the more impatient of the two. He remembered the many times when Diamond-Back had acted beyond discretion; how he didn't like to sit things out for very long. It was important that the nerves of one of them should reach the snapping point.

It was Diamond-Back who did it. Clay saw Diamond-Back's dark skin stretch tight and flat across his face, and his teeth make a narrow rip of his mouth, like he couldn't keep the tension in him any longer for the thinking of it. He saw Diamond-Back make a slow hunch forward, and fork his hand down, and heard the high trees receive the guns' shouting and slam it back upon the forest carpet from their crowns.

He was aware of Ygenio beside him in a half-crouch with his hand working the heavy-barreled Colt and his hat all the way off now, like a bullet had maybe snatched it from his head. And he was conscious of his own firing, of the butt riding fat and solid in his hand and of the bullets tearing big and heavy into Robey Moore, and lifting him and taking him into the woodpile and turning him again and carrying him into Diamond-Back, who was firing wildly from his knees, with the muzzle of his gun aimed at everything and nothing.

And when the slug took him in the shoulder he didn't feel the pain of it, but just the soft-hard jarring and the sense of being pushed back, and he kept on firing at Robey until the gun was empty, and only when he tried to walk toward Robey's fallen body did he find he couldn't move; and he said quietly, amazedly, 'Good Christ!'

Then Ygenio had him under the other arm, and around his middle, and was talking to him in a rapid flow of words and laughing softly and far away. Ygenio's voice was coming to him on undulating waves, like the ripples of a creek or brook.

'*Amigo, amigo,*' he was saying, 'Clay, it is done now, look how it is done, it is *magnífico. Amigo*, we have done what we have come to do—it is accomplished. See, how everything is finished.'

And Clay leaned on Ygenio and felt the strength and reality of Ygenio supporting him erect. He saw Diamond-Back and Robey lying smashed and twisted in the woodpile in the silence of the clearing where the cabin stood. For a great while it was the vastest silence he had ever heard; a total silence without any kind of sound to break it.

Then, way far off, the squirrel made a tentative sort of noise. And the jay bird came down and flipped its wings in shadows across the sun-lit ground.

16

In the first days of returning to the *casas* of Ygenio's relatives, Clay was in the hands of the old Raphael, who consigned him to a narrow bed in a *yeso*-plastered room, and devoted endless hours to the treatment of the shoulder wound.

His old *mamacita*—glory to her bones— had been a *curandera* in her lifetime and she had entrusted the secrets of her many herbs and cures to him before her passing. Such an unhappy thing as this wounding of the young *señor* would give him an opportunity to refresh his memory and skill in the healing arts, and also it would keep him out of those ferocious arguments they were having in the evening.

A person with the responsibilities of a *curandera* could not afford to dally with tequila and the stupid politics of those who herded sheep. The young *señor* was fortunate indeed to have such a skillful person at his bedside. It was true the wound was clean, but without the ministrations of one who knew his craft the young *señor* might well become the object of grief and wailing at a *velorio del defunto*. One could not be too careful; no, one could not.

So, Clay lay in the yeso-plastered room without objection, and let the easy life of Raphael's household flow around him. It was a pleasurable existence that appealed to him during the time that he was immobilized, and since they'd stopped the arguing in the evenings out of deference to him there were no longer the loud haranguings to disturb him.

In his own case there was a division of labor in effect so flattering that Ygenio held it would surely spoil him for the rigors which might befall his life when all the attention would have to end. And while Clay appreciated the implied danger of this indolence himself, it was nice to have

Apolinaria cooking for him and bringing his meals to him especially in his room; to have Abrana washing out his clothes and mending them and smiling at him as she did so; and even to have the children visit him from time to time and whisper, '*muy valiente*,' to one another as their wondering eyes memorized the details of him lying there. And then old Raphael coming with his herbs again.

Such a thing could spoil a man for life—Ygenio was right, Almost made him want to get himself all shot up again.

But there were times of being alone in solitude when he would feel a disturbing tide of spirit, even though he knew he couldn't do much yet. He would be gazing idly out the window, or contemplating the honest, homely beauty of the *santo* on the wall before him, or perhaps the carvings of the old *trastero* leaning in its corner, when, of a sudden, he'd see the riders coming up the alley to the ranch, and the men stomping on the gallery and the thin light coming from the dark room.

And he would feel the rigidity which this thinking was inducing in him, and he would know that everything was not finished with that business yet.

By the time a week had passed and he was allowed to move about it was especially that way, and more and more his mind would speculate on what was happening in the valley. He could spend long hours in a small and sun-lit court now, enjoying the yellow torching of the aspens and the brilliant scarlet of the drying peppers hanging from the *vigas*, but these diversions could not keep his mind away from the valley very long. He grew increasingly impatient to learn what was going on down there.

On the third day of this basking in the autumn sun Ygenio came to him and perched on the edge of the wooden tub where Abrana had been washing clothes.

'I know what you are thinking, and I fix it,' Ygenio said. 'Soon we know how things are going down there. I have sent Jesus down to look around.'

'What?' Clay said. That name always startled him, even though the Spanish way with it was different.

'Jesus,' Ygenio said. 'The young son of Lorenzo, who argues so much. He has gone to Roswell to see how things are for us; he should be back in a day or two.'

'I hope he's careful down there,' Clay said. 'I hope he keeps his mouth shut.'

'He will be all right,' Ygenio said. 'He is not like Lorenzo; he will be careful, and quiet, too.' Ygenio watched the slight movement of the pepper *ristras* on the *vigas*. 'Do you feel better now? Raphael said that you are coming fine. He said you can go almost any time now.'

Clay moved the injured shoulder with a slow, circular movement of his arm. 'It feels pretty good,' he said. 'I think it's healed inside all right; it's mostly stiffness now. I think this sun is good for it.'

'Yes, the sun is very good,' Ygenio said. 'The sun will help a lot. It will make it fine.'

Clay watched the aspens moving in the breeze. 'I don't like to be so much trouble,' he said. 'I'm putting everyone out around here.'

'Yes, you are a great burden,' Ygenio said, and he cocked his head to one side and winked at Abrana as she came from the *casa* with one of Clay's shirts. 'Is that no so, *muchacha*? How easy it would be otherwise.'

'What is that?' Abrana said. She stopped beside Clay's chair and looked at the bandage which covered the shoulder.

'I simply say that Clay is a great burden.'

'Yes,' Abrana said. 'It would be much easier if he had been killed up there with the others.' She said it with a straight face, but there was mirth watching from her eyes.

'Then you would have had to bury three of us,' Clay said. 'How does that strike you?'

'That I had not thought of,' Ygenio admitted, and he laughed. 'So you are a care any way it is observed.'

'Yes—just look at this shirt,' Abrana said. She showed Clay the frayed collar and the rent in the cloth where the bullet had torn through it. 'It made me ill to wash this; do you wish me to mend it for you?'

Clay looked at Abrana without bothering to

examine the damage. He was enjoying this conversation and he felt like playing with her. 'Why not? What's the matter with it? Can't you fix a little thing like that?'

'Of course, but I do not like this one. You should get rid of it. I do not like to think about it.'

Abrana's face had changed again and Clay could see that she was no longer fooling with him. She was serious about the shirt.

'All right,' he said. 'Throw it out.'

'I will burn it,' Abrana said. 'I would rather burn it than throw it out,' and she rolled it up and put it beneath her arm. 'We will be eating soon,' she went on when neither of them said anything but simply laughed. 'Will albondigas and enchiladas be all right?'

'Of course,' Ygenio said. 'Anything to avoid starvation. But make it soon.'

It was clear that Ygenio was feeling good, and Clay fell into his patois. 'Yes, we are becoming skin and bones.'

'It will be soon enough,' Abrana said. 'You take the sun a while longer,' she added; and she went inside again.

'You see?' Ygenio said. 'They are very complicated.'

Clay waited before he spoke again. He'd been thinking about this new thing and he'd been waiting for a chance to spring it on Ygenio. Now that he was well again this was a good time. He wanted to do this thing before

216

they left for home.

'How far to Lincoln?' he asked Ygenio.

'Oh, a few miles. We are maybe as many miles to Lincoln as to Hondo. It is not far. Why do you ask?'

'I was wondering if you'd take a run up there.'

'Of course. But for what?'

'I want you to see the Padre.'

'The Padre?' Ygenio's puzzlement made shaggy arches of his eyebrows.

'At San Juan,' Clay said. He was grinning broadly at Ygenio. 'The Padre at San Juan. The church.'

'Oh ho.' Ygenio said it slowly, in an exhalation. 'So that is it. Oh ho.'

'What's the matter? Didn't you think I'd do it? What do you think I am?'

'Well, I was wondering,' Ygenio said. 'Of course, I will go, if you are serious.'

'I'm serious, all right. Do you like it?'

'Yes, I like it all right. I think it will be very fine.' Ygenio's eyes were partly closed in humor and the wrinkles fanned out from them in fine lines.

'All right,' Clay said. 'If you'll take care of the details it will help.'

'It will be a pleasure,' Ygenio said. 'I will see when he can do it. Will we go back then?'

'Yes,' Clay said. 'But I want to do this first. I think it's better than waiting until we get home. We don't know what might be waiting

217

for us down there.'

'No,' Ygenio said, 'but we will find out. It will be nice to have it here, though. Yes, it will be very nice.'

*   *   *

Young Jesus, the son of Lorenzo, returned on the third day and Ygenio brought him around to the court where Clay was lying on a blanket watching Abrana wash his one remaining shirt. He was bare to the waist, and lying on his back, but when Ygenio brought the boy through the door he sat up and smiled. Abrana turned away from the tub at the sound of the entry and when she saw Clay smiling she asked, 'What are you laughing at?'

'Nothing in particular,' Clay said to her. 'I was just thinking how nice it is to have you do for me like this.'

Abrana squeezed the water from the shirt and held it up to look at it. 'It will not always be this way,' she said. 'At home you will have more shirts to wear.'

'I had another here until you burned it,' Clay said. 'You brought this on yourself.' He found this domestic life highly amusing, so far.

'I would rather wash this one every day than wash that one once a month. That one had bad memories.'

When Abrana took the shirt to a line she had strung Ygenio and Jesus came to the blanket and squatted at the edge of it.

'Are we interrupting something?' Ygenio said.

'No,' Clay told him. 'That's all right. We were just talking about that shirt again.'

'I thought it was burned. Is it resurrected?'

'Yes,' Clay said. 'It won't stay dead.'

'You will get used to each other,' Ygenio said, and he was laughing quietly.

The young Jesus fingered the brim of his wide hat until Clay spoke to him. He was a slight person with thin features and a mole on the bridge of his nose which made him appear crosseyed sometimes.

'What did you find out down there?' Clay said. 'Did you go to the ranch?'

'Yes. I went to the town first, and then the ranch,' Jesus said. 'It was quiet in the ranch, and no one was there.'

'All right; that's good. What could you find out in town? Were they hunting for us?'

'No,' Jesus said. 'In a cantina I learn that they go to your place only the one time, and not beyond that. The one with whom you fight has gone unmourned.'

'That ain't surprisin',' Clay said.

'No, he does not sound like one who would be greatly missed,' Ygenio said.

'But I think there are those who wait for you to return,' Jesus said. 'I am not sure of that, for it is hard for one like me to learn things, but that is what I think. From small

219

words dropped here and there.'

'You did all right,' Clay said. 'You did fine. I guess we can head down, then, Ygenio. There'll likely be trouble, but I guess we can handle it.'

'It cannot be much worse than what we already have,' Ygenio said, and laughed. 'So we might as well.'

Abrana was listening to this, but she waited until Ygenio and Jesus had gone into the *casa* before she came to the blanket and sat with Clay.

'Do you think it is safe down there now?' she asked.

'As safe as it'll ever be, I guess,' Clay said. He thought before he continued. Then he said, 'Ygenio saw the Padre up at Lincoln. Up at San Juan.'

'The Padre?' Abrana said. 'Has he sinned again?'

'Probably, but this was different. He went for me, and you. It would be a nice church to get married in.'

'Oh?' Abrana was smiling at the trees above.

'Yes. Is that all right up there? It won't be fancy, but I don't mind, if you don't.'

'I think it will be fine,' Abrana said. She stopped and looked at him again. 'Are you certain of this?'

'Sure, I'm certain,' Clay said. 'Don't you think I am? I wouldn't ask you if I wasn't.'

She was laughing as she answered. 'I know that. Yes, I believe you are sure of it. I do not want you to regret it later. Do not become excited.'

'I ain't excited. You're sure you'll like it at San Juan?'

'It will be very beautiful,' Abrana said. She leaned across and kissed him lightly on the cheek; and laughed again.

'You are so solemn,' she said to him. 'Are all men solemn at such a time?'

'I don't know,' Clay said. 'I ain't solemn; I'm just gettin' used to it. Ygenio said it takes a while.'

'Did he? What else did he say?' Her cheeks were tight with smiling at him.

'That's between us,' Clay said, and grinned at her. 'Men can't tell everything they know. Look, is tomorrow all right? Will you have something to wear?'

'Yes, tomorrow is all right,' Abrana said. 'I will find a dress here. Does that make a difference?'

'Not for me. I just want it nice for you. I always thought women liked to make a grand thing of it.'

'You will make it grand for me. A dress will not change anything, but I will find one. Will Ygenio be with you?'

'I guess so,' Clay said. 'We ought to have Apolinaria, and Raphael, too. For you.'

'All right. Raphael will like that. He has

221

been very good to us. But we will keep it simple.'

'Yes,' Clay said. 'That's a good idea.'

*　　　*　　　*

Ygenio had the rig hitched to the buckskin mare in the morning and they were all to ride in that except for Raphael, who was pleased to accompany them upon the red roan horse. It was to be a simple thing, but already the other members of the household had gone on to Lincoln by whatever means they could, and Raphael was resplendent in the antique trappings of a don. It seemed to Clay that Raphael had kept those garments in his vast, carved chest since the time of Coronado; but he was very elegant and lent a dash of grandeur.

Clay rode in the front seat beside Ygenio, and Abrana was with Apolinaria behind them. Apolinaria was not so sure that Clay should be allowed to see Abrana before the ceremony, but there was no avoiding it and Clay thought she looked very beautiful and radiant in the ancient ivory dress and lace mantilla she had borrowed from one of the other women. He had borrowed tailored trousers and a hand-stitched Spanish shirt himself, but he felt drab in comparison to all this splendor.

It was all arranged beforehand and there was no confusion when they came to the church and Ygenio halted the rig, and they all stepped down. He and Clay went in ahead to the Padre, who was waiting for them, and when Abrana came in with Apolinaria and Raphael, Ygenio introduced them.

'This is the Señorita Abrana Martinez, and the Señor Clay Forrest,' he explained formally.

Abrana inclined her head to the Padre and Clay shook hands with him, and said uncertainly, 'How do you do?'

The thin man with the beaked nose and heavy eyebrows, which seemed out of proportion to the rest of his face, took Clay's hand and said, *'Buenos días*, Señor Forrest.' Then he took his book in both hands and looked at Ygenio.

'Are you with them?' he said.

'Yes,' Ygenio said. 'And these two, as well.' He indicated Raphael and Apolinaria.

'Very well.' The Padre cleared his throat, and commenced to read.

Clay and Abrana stood quietly beside each other as this was going on, and Clay was conscious of the silence accentuating the words which the Padre spoke to them. Many people had come into the church before or after them, but they were very still, and because of this the soundlessness was further intensified.

But Clay wasn't thinking of what the Padre was reading from his book, but of all things

223

which had led him to this moment in his life. He was thinking what an odd coincidence it was that this ceremony should occur in the same town where so many bad and evil things had happened to him. Through an open window he could see the drowsy town and the street where the Ellis House was standing, and he remembered the day he'd listened to the old guy on the veranda and the moment of recognition when he'd run from there and had surrendered himself to Peppin.

And he could see the courthouse building, the old Murphy Big Store, and the high outside staircase leading to the second floor where he was kept in jail until the trial. There was a window up there in which he used to stand and look out upon the street, and he remembered that, after he had gone from there to prison, there was a story telling how Billy Bonney had finally been arrested for his part in Sheriff Brady's killing, and he, too, had been accustomed to standing in that window. And the story told that one day he'd added another chapter to his growing legend by killing a guard named Bell and another one named Ollinger, and had then escaped. But Pat Garret had got him in the end.

But this was only a part of it. The rest was of his family and how it would be if they had lived for this. The idea of this would be something for his pa to get accustomed to, and he thought it would be easier for his ma because she was God-loving as well as God-fearing, and would not complicate things the way his pa might be inclined to do. But it would be all right with both of them. And Rusty should be here, too.

Then it was interrupted for him and the Padre was asking for the ring, and Ygenio gave Clay the one which Raphael had made and Clay slipped it on Abrana's finger. After that he held her hand while the Padre made the last pronouncements, and then he kissed her when the Padre closed the book.

'Thank you very much,' Clay shook hands with the Padre who smiled and shook hands with Abrana, too, and then the others. 'That was very nice.'

'Yes,' Abrana said. 'It was beautiful. Thank you.'

When the Padre said good-bye to them they went outside again and got into the rig and Ygenio started off. Apolinaria sat beside him this time and Clay was in the back with Abrana, and he was conscious of her smiling at him, and the warm, possessive feeling that it made in him.

'Are you satisfied now?' Clay said to her.

'It was your idea, but it's nice.'

'You'll get used to it,' Clay said. He was thinking of Ygenio's remark, and he laughed.

'What were you thinking of?' Abrana said. 'I was watching you. You were far away.'

'I was just down the street, here,' Clay said.

'I wasn't so far. I was just thinking of everything, I guess.'

'I was, too,' Abrana said. 'I do not think that anybody listens. It is too much the beginning and the end of everything.'

'Yes,' Clay said, 'like dying,' and they laughed together.

Clay became more aware of the people on the streets who were watching them. Once again he remembered how it had been before when he was in this town and he wondered which of those out there now had been his enemies, and which might still be, for all he knew. Going past the courthouse, one of those standing on the stairway called to him and he recognized a jailer who had been in charge of him.

'Hey, Forrest!'

Clay found him on the stairway. He wondered if something was going to start again. 'What do you want?' he called. He felt belligerent.

'What you doin' here?'

'Gettin' married.' Clay felt foolish calling this in front of everyone, but it was obvious.

'Married?' The jailer was leaning on the railing, trying to hear.

'Yeah. Do you mind?'

'Not at all,' the jailer's voice came back to him. He was farther away by now. 'Good luck!'

'Thanks,' Clay shouted to him; and then he removed his hat and waved it.

226

17

The stiffness of the shoulder, not so apparent when Clay was sitting around at Raphael's, deviled him all the way down from that place to the Pecos valley country. Riding horseback for long stretches was a different thing altogether from lying in the sun upon his back; and though Abrana perceived this as well as he, and insisted that they pause a day at the jacal of a herder where they'd stayed the one night during the journey, he refused to listen to this logic, and led them hurrying on.

They had been away for long enough and the nearer he got to home the more anxious he became. He wanted to get this business over with.

Anything happening now was going to be anticlimatic, but he wanted to see it finished. There was going to be some kind of trouble down there, and it didn't make much difference that Jesus' observations had implied a placid atmosphere. But he didn't give a damn about it now. After Robey and the old crowd, he could laugh at all of them.

He still had a sort of wonder in him when he thought of that much of it being done and over with, but he was getting used to it. He had only to look at Abrana riding next to him and understand what that implied, or at

227

Apolinaria, whose face was emanating pleasure despite her sitting on a horse again, to know that something good was happening and that the bad things, or anyway, the worst of them, were over with. He was going to start to live now; the way a man had really ought to live.

He led them down the Hondo into Roswell. He was eager to get going at the ranch again, but he didn't wish to start in there until everything was squared away with the people down in town. If there was any trouble to be had he wanted to initiate it, and not go slinking out to his place and let them come out and hunt for him again. He had in mind to tell them how the end had come to Robey Moore, and that they'd never have to gun up on his account again. He'd like to do that in a peaceful manner, if they'd let him, but they could have it any way they wanted it. He hadn't forgotten Chandler, and the Gallaghers, and others who might be hot for him; nearly anything could happen. But it didn't bother him.

There had been a light rain the night before and the air was clean and washed above the valley when they came in sight of it in the morning. There was no dust anywhere and they could look straight on out until the earth curved down and there was nothing any more to see. The Pecos had a glimmer to it in the sun, and the irrigation ditches were winding through the fields like some of Raphael's delicate silver wires.

When they came down through the last of the fields at the edge of the town and entered the street Clay became aware again of the many people everywhere. Every time he'd thought of that in other days, the *extranjeros* he'd never seen before, and the village bursting up like some exotic plant, he'd had a kind of resentment in him; but that was all changed now, and he had the feeling that he'd have to view the place with tolerance because the growth of it into something big and vital would affect him and everything he had. He couldn't be so much of a separate entity any more. Just so he didn't have to be in the middle of it, it would be all right. So long as he was sitting prosperous out there nothing any more could bother him.

Halfway down this street Clay saw Old Man Medford and the Gallaghers and Jack Harris and several others standing near the hotel gallery, and that was all right, too. Those people were watching in a way that made him think they might have seen him from a long way off, and had gathered together like that to take their council. Someone had likely spotted them coming in along the long slopes over west, but that was nothing to worry over. Clay and Ygenio went right up to those standing round about; he didn't care.

'Hello, Medford,' Clay said. 'I come back
229

again. I got a notion you didn't expect me to. But here I am.'

Old Man Medford turned a tobacco plug over in his mouth. Clay thought his bold approach might have made them wonder. He knew they saw his travel stains and the odd way in which he held his arm, and he thought they might be wary about what was going to happen now.

'Well, I see you are back, Clay,' Old Man Medford said. 'You sure are, ain't you? Can't say as we did expect you. Not after you lit out the way you did.'

'I had a lot to do and I couldn't stay around,' Clay said. 'We been up in the Capitans doin' your law work for you. Me an' Ygenio, here, done for Robey and his crowd.'

Medford's face became a blank. 'Done for Robey?'

'Uh huh,' Clay said. 'Him and Diamond-Back and Ed Picket and Steve Howard. Would have got Fergus, too, but Robey done it for us. You ain't got much to worry about from them any more.'

Steve Gallagher edged out to one side. 'How do we know that's straight, Forrest? We took a lot from them. How do we know?' Clay knew Steve Gallagher was still thinking about the Pine Tree iron.

'Best go see for yourself,' Clay said to him. 'Howard and Picket're buried over near Encinosa—I'll tell you the place when you want to go. Robey and Diamond-Back're up near Bowdre's old place on the Ruidoso. There's a cabin up there, with a woodpile next to it; they're under that.'

'We could not bury those two as nicely as we wished,' Ygenio said. 'There were difficulties.'

Old Man Medford relaxed a little. 'I guess you did do for 'em, didn't you?'

'We done it, all right,' Clay said. He felt good talking to these men this way. 'They shot Rusty Rhodes the day I left. Something had to give.'

'Rhodes?'

'Uh huh. Rusty Rhodes, Medford. In the back. There weren't many like him.'

Clay gathered his reins when Apolinaria and Abrana came up behind them. As the men removed their hats, Clay moved the roan to make room for Abrana, and introduced her to them as his wife.

'How do you do?' they said together.

'Very well, thank you,' Abrana said, and she smiled at them with pleasure, and not shyness. 'I am happy to know you.'

'Why, thank you very much,' Old Man Medford said, and he blinked. 'You got a lot done on your trip, didn't you, Clay?'

'Well, that's true, all right,' Clay said. 'We're goin' up home now. If there's any settlin' to be done you know where to find me. I'm thinkin' you may want me for trial on that shootin'. I'll stand it if you want me to. I was in the right.'

'Ain't everybody hated you, Clay,' Jack Harris said. 'Most was mixed up, is all. Scared-like. Most know you shot in self-defense, them as saw it. They'll speak for you. I will.'

Clay felt a pretty good feeling coming into him. 'Thanks, Jack,' he said. 'Maybe we ought to have a trial just the same. Keep the town from gettin' dull.'

'Fat chance of that,' Jack Harris said, and Harris was smiling now, and so were a lot of others.

Old Man Medford took hold of Clay's bridle and looked up at him. 'Clay,' he said, 'Dodge is out to your place today. Him and Sam Chandler. Dodge didn't figure on your coming back, and he's taking himself an inventory.'

'Inventory? What for? He don't own it.'

'No, but he figured he might some day. He wanted to know what to bid when the place went up for taxes.'

'Is that so?' Clay looked down the street. The rain had laid the dust, but it was picking up again. In a busy town like this one it wouldn't ever stay down. 'Dodge, huh? Well, I'll see about him. And Chandler, too.'

'You be careful of them two,' Old Man Medford said. 'We got Sam here to help out, but he's taken a shine to Dodge's business. You want us to come along?'

'No, that's all right,' Clay said. 'It ain't goin'

to be anything like that. I'm through with that. I'll just talk to 'em.'

He moved ahead a few paces, and Abrana came up beside him. 'You do as he said, Clay,' she said to him. 'You be careful out there. You do not act simply for yourself any more.'

'I know that,' Clay said, and he smiled at her. 'I'll remember. You and Apolinaria better stay here for a while. Until we come and get you.'

'No,' Abrana said. 'We will come, but we will follow at a distance. Do you mind that?'

Clay turned it over in his mind. 'No,' he said. 'That's all right, I guess.' Then, as Ygenio joined him, he turned around again. 'If any of you fellers want to come on out some time, you're welcome to. And bring your missus. We got a good view out there.'

*   *   *

They left the women coming at a slower pace, and proceeded at a gallop. Shortly out of town, the land began to lift and in a little while Clay could see the cottonwoods leading to the buildings; and then he lost them for a time as the incline intervened to obscure his vision. He was coming home again and he felt that he would never get there. The one look was a tantalizing thing and it seemed that he would never get another. But they were coming home and they hadn't far to go.

233

Coming up the winding valley road, and breaking out upon the level land on top, Clay saw Chandler lounging at the entrance of the tree lane, leading in. His horse was grazing off a distance and Chandler was sitting on a flat rock with a cigarette in his hand. It made him angry to think of Chandler taking his ease, unruffled-like, and yet he didn't want to get involved in a lot of shooting any more. A man like Chandler had to have a lesson, though— the kind that he would not forget. Something that would maybe drive him out and shame him into another country altogether.

By the time he had a scheme hatched they were getting closer and Chandler was looking at them with attentiveness. They hadn't slowed like Chandler maybe thought they ought to, out of deference to him, and Clay could tell he was getting nervous. He didn't think that Chandler recognized them yet, but he knew that he was getting jumpy just the same. Less than a hundred yards away, Chandler squashed his cigarette and shaded his eyes in their direction; then he turned and ran for the rifle sticking from his saddle scabbard.

Clay's arm hurt like hell, but he shook a loop into his riata anyway. It was maybe a dangerous thing to undertake, but he knew what he was going to do with Chandler now and he had to take the chance. He'd been confused about that man—kind of hard to tell if he was really bad, or just an imitation—but he had his mind made up and he was going to act accordingly. Men like Chandler had to learn their manners now and then; they had to be deflated.

Chandler nearly got them with the rifle. He jerked it out and swerved around just as Clay swung his loop and let it go. Clay could see Sam's face and the quick fear leaping into it as he got a good look at the men coming at him. Then the loop settled low around his knees and Clay dogged the end around his saddle horn, and kept the horse moving onward. When the slack ran out Chandler made an acrobatic flip in the air and landed on his back.

By the time Clay freed the riata from the horn and got down, Ygenio was bending over Chandler, laughing softly. Chandler lay in the grass with his arms wide and his eyes closed in his white face.

'Is he breathing?' Clay said. Chandler had a dead look.

'Oh, yes,' Ygenio said. 'He is breathing, and he has a fine heartbeat; but he is sleeping very soundly.'

'Just as well,' Clay said. Clay coiled the riata and gave it to Ygenio. 'You might tie this bird up and drape him in his saddle.'

'Shall I send him back to town?'

'All right.' Clay turned his head and looked up the alley toward a bend, far down. 'On the other hand, wait a bit. Maybe we can send Dodge along with him. They came out together; they might as well go back that way.'

'Shall I tie him and come with you?' Ygenio said. 'That Dodge, he is a strange one; you can never tell about him.'

'No. That's all right. He ain't even goin' to get a look at me. Give me five minutes, then squeeze a round off in the air. I want him lookin' this way.'

Ygenio took out his tobacco and began to roll a smoke. 'All right. I will wait here, then. I will shoot the gun for you, too. It is nice here in the sun. Be careful, though.'

Clay got his rifle from the roan horse and walked up the lane. Just before the bend he turned off, cutting through the brush and undergrowth, going quietly. He knew that Dodge would be keeping a wary eye upon things, and that the shot out front would alert him good. He had a special kind of treatment in his mind for Dodge, and he didn't want anything to spoil it.

He moved through the brush slow and silent. He kept down low and went ahead in short movements from one clump of cover to the next. When he came around to the side of the house he heard the shot, distant, but clear, and he backed off some and worked up a small rise of ground, and hunkered down behind a low rock. From that place, maybe thirty feet from the house, he could see through the side window into the big main room. He knew Dodge had heard the shot because the big man was squatting down behind a front window with his pistol out, looking up the cottonwood lane.

Dodge was maybe fifty feet away from Clay, his back nearly toward him, and he fit into the rifle sights very well. Clay moved them up and down his body, looking for a good spot. Dodge was so fat and round he couldn't hardly miss, but he knew it'd have to be the best shooting that he'd ever done. There couldn't be anything slipshod about this piece of work.

It made him wish he had Pa's old Ballard out there with him. You couldn't hardly beat a Winchester for most things, but he wished he had the Ballard just the same. That gun had a special set of sights, and Hardin had taught him mark-shooting with it; there wasn't any gun that could beat it for a thing like this. You could give a man a shave with that old gun, one skinny whisker at a time.

He kept looking for a good place. The sun coming into that room shone on every part of Dodge, and he could have his choice. Dodge's thick neck made tanned rolls above his collar, and his big backsides rounded out behind him like the mountain moon. Dodge was wearing light-colored pants today, which made his rear end bigger still.

Clay scrunched lower on the ground. He got his elbows in solid and felt the stock press

237

smooth and tight against his cheek. There was just the faintest smell of oil about the action, and the sun made a glint on the barrel where the bluing had worn away; he'd have to fix that some time.

He put a slow pressure on the trigger, and increased it. He took one last breath, then let it out slow. At the bottom of it he pulled the trigger; he pulled it right on through the crack of sound.

Dodge Liston jumped. Dodge Liston jumped like some kind of a cat, a scalded cat. He leaped straight up in the air and he went forward through the front window all in one motion, and he lit running, with the glass flying and his fat knees pumping and both hands clamped to his wide bottom. He moved so fast it was slightly unbelievable, certainly a spectacle to marvel at, and Clay just could see where the pants were burned in a long, straight line.

Then Dodge was in the dooryard and moving out. He didn't even stop to get his horse, but kept pounding up the lane. He raised a small spine of dust all the way up to the bend and out of sight.

Clay came slowly down and stood in the sun. He didn't want to go inside just yet. He was thinking that he ought to wait until Abrana got there before he did that; maybe even ought to carry her across the doorway. He'd heard that was the proper thing to do.

It was nice standing there and waiting. He could feel the promise of its permanence hard against his boot-soles; and it was in the air, too, where he could breathe it. No more leaving this place now. No more riding night trails in the mountains. No more anything like that.

He sat on the gallery and looked up the lane. Ygenio'd have Dodge on his way back to town now, if Dodge hadn't run it all the way. And Chandler would be going with him. Pretty soon the others would be coming up, and in a while they'd have a feed. Golly, he was hungry.

He leaned against a post and closed his eyes. A faint pain pulsed in his shoulder, but the sun was warm and he didn't care about that slight annoyance. It was nice being like this and nothing mattered.

When he looked again he saw Ygenio's faceless figure waiting at the alley bend. He saw Ygenio taking off his hat and waving it, like a shadow thrown against a wall. Clay rose from the gallery and started walking out to meet them. In another moment he saw the other horses coming through the trees, pieces of them first, and not complete because the branches and the trunks were obscuring them. As he entered the alley he recognized Apolinaria's shapelessness at the bend upon the gentle buckskin mare, her features shaded by the boughs.

239

When Ygenio moved again there was room for all of them to ride abreast, and Clay saw the third horse join the others. They were silhouettes, still, but a few yards on the sun came through a break in the branches and he could see their faces clearly. He could see Abrana coming home.